CW00736165

SOUL CATCHER

A SHADOW DETECTIVE NOVEL

WILLIAM MASSA

CRITICAL MASS PUBLISHING

Copyright © 2017 by WILLIAM MASSA

All rights reserved.

No part of this book may be reproduced in any form or by any electronic or mechanical means, including information storage and retrieval systems, without written permission from the author, except for the use of brief quotations in a book review.

Want to get a FREE NOVELLA?

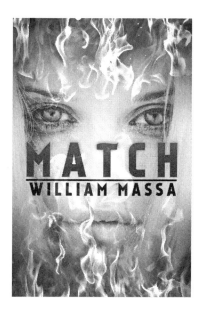

A CHILLING GHOST STORY!
Not everyone you meet online is who they claim to be.
Sometimes they may not even be alive...
Mark found her photo on a popular dating app. Her name was Akasha, and she was beautiful. Seductive. Irresistible. She wrote that she was

looking for friendship. Love. A real connection. But Akasha is concealing a terrifying secret...

Jon my newsletter and receive a free book. Emails will be infrequent, spam free and deal only with new books, special offers, etc. **Sign up here** . **If you do I will send you a copy of for FREE.**

1

Anxiety churned deep inside the pit of Joe Cormac's stomach, and he wished he had never signed up for this crazy ghost-hunting expedition. Hell, he would have almost preferred to be back in Iraq instead of squeezed into an equipment-stuffed van alongside a team of parapsychologists gearing up for a paranormal investigation.

Two men in their late twenties, scruffy scientist types, flanked their more refined-looking leader. Steve —bald, Dominican, with a double chin—and Nick— wild mop of curly hair and an equally frizzy beard— formed a protective circle around Dr. Michelle Gould. The fair-skinned, raven-haired leader of the trio of ghost chasers was in her mid-forties, a former Goth girl turned student of the weird. The emerald eyes framed by a pair of large, round glasses shone with an intellectual excitement that stood in sharp contrast to Joe's grim-faced expression of unease. Dr. Gould loved hunting ghosts and probing the mysteries of the beyond. The paranormal was her calling. For Joe, it felt more like a curse.

Unlike Gould and her two assistants, Joe had not chosen this path in life. It had been thrust upon him. Shrapnel from an IED back in Iraq had nearly killed him. Correction, it *did* kill him. But when the medics brought him back, Joe was...different. It wasn't just the scars covering his torso, either. He was able to see the souls of the dead.

Dr. Gould's words rang out in his mind for the hundredth time:

"You survived for a reason, Joe. I truly believe that. You've been given a special gift."

Joe didn't feel so special at this moment. He felt scared.

The van came to a sudden, grinding halt. They'd reached their destination: Club Link. There had been six deaths at the club in the last three months. Cops shut the place down when a couple was found in the basement with their necks snapped. According to eyewitness accounts, a spectral figure had been spotted in the club that same night. It was just one of many sightings since the strange string of deaths. The police naturally ignored those reports, but they'd gotten Gould's full attention.

"Two months ago, a model overdosed at Club Link. I believe she is our lady in white," Dr. Gould said, unable to hide her growing excitement.

At times like these, Joe called her "Dr. Ghoul," if not aloud. What demons drove the parapsychologists? Why would someone voluntarily seek out spirits and face down the supernatural? Every time the question came up, she skillfully changed the subject. The parapsychologist remained a mystery to him. Mind reading wasn't among Joe's psychic abilities, so all he could do was speculate. Something had set Gould on her current journey. And perhaps it was best if he didn't know what exactly fueled her unusual obsession.

Dr. Gould nodded at Steve to open the van door. Biting night air greeted them, and Joe's teeth chattered as he wrapped his arms tighter around his upper body.

One by one, they got out of the van and were joined by Tony, the driver. He was a long beanpole of a man decked out in a Navy wool peacoat that looked a hell of a lot warmer than Joe's flimsy leather jacket.

"If the reports are to be believed, we're dealing with an entity that has no problem lashing out against the living," Gould said. "Based on the profile we put together, Selina

Hill was a troubled young woman. The poor girl struggled with bipolar episodes and a string of other mental health issues, which probably accounts for her heavy drug use. In life, she was confused and angry; in death, she has become a danger to others. She needs our help."

"Hey, she sounds just like your type," Steve said to Tony, elbowing him with a grin. The tall parapsychologist shot him a withering look. Dr. Gould rolled her eyes, her impatience palpable. This wasn't the time for jokes. Her voice was empty of all humor as she continued the briefing. "Keep your guard up and stay close to Joe. He's the only one who can actually see what might be lurking within those walls."

The team's expectant eyes bored into him and his hands shook with the pressure of having to live up to his reputation. Even though he had only participated in two other ghost hunts before, they all saw him as some psychic superhero. Joe felt more like a man in over his head. Helping the dead was the right thing to do, but interpreting readings on a bunch of instruments was a lot less terrifying than staring into the envious eyes of a forsaken soul yearning to be alive again.

Dammit, I never wanted any of this!

Why had he let Gould talk him into this latest spook adventure?

Sometimes Joe wished that the IED had just finished him that day. Shame washed over him as soon as the dark thought slashed through his mind. Maybe Dr. Gould was right. Maybe he survived the blast that killed the rest of his unit for a reason. In a way, he felt like he was honoring his fallen brothers every time he successfully used his powers.

His breath steadying, he took in the ominous warehouse-turned-nightclub before him. Death was waiting for him inside, of that he was certain. On a normal night, muscle-bound bouncers would front long lines of club-goers while thumping techno boomed down the street. Today the structure stood abandoned, and an eerie silence permeated the block.

Joe trailed the team of ghost hunters. Dr. Gould briskly strode toward the structure, confident as ever. Tony, Nick and Steve marched behind her, troops following their general into battle.

A nerve twinged in the back of Joe's neck as he fell farther behind the scientists. *Dammit*, the pressure of the situation was getting to him. Most spirits were lost, confused and essentially harmless. But other ghosts envied the living. Determined to remain on this plane, their sole pleasure came from inflicting misery and pain. If the murders were any indication, the ghost of the dead model appeared to fall into a different category.

Tony stepped up to the club's steel door and pulled it open with a loud metallic screech that sent jarring vibrations up Joe's spine. Moments later, they switched on their flashlights and entered the reception area. Joe drew a small sense of comfort from the thin beam of light emanating from his hand. Heart pounding, he swept his light over the coat-check room next to the box office and then a second door leading deeper into the shadowy club.

Nick whipped out an electrostatic locator and an electromagnetic field detector—classic ghostbusting equipment. One device measured ionization while the other could detect changes in the electromagnetic field. It was all pseudo-scientific gobbledygook to Joe. The only instrument he needed were the eyes he was born with and the psychic sensitivity triggered by his near-death experience. Beyond the next doorway was the spacious dance floor. Flashlights raked the darkness, revealing steel cages suspended from the ceiling that were normally occupied by undulating go-go dancers. Nearby stairs led to a series of catwalks overlooking the dance floor.

As the team started to fan out, Dr. Gould continued to radiate a mixture of tension and excitement. Her flashlight mapping the way, she surged toward the winding staircase leading to dance floors on the second and third level of the structure. Joe had visited enough clubs back in his day to know each room probably catered to a different type of music, when the club was in operation.

"Is anyone here?" Dr. Gould asked eagerly.

The question hung in the air.

"We know you're upset. Alone. Confused."

More silence.

"We're here to help you," Gould said. "We mean you no harm."

We may not mean the ghost any harm, but did the dead model feel the same way?

Renewed silence.

Joe sighed inwardly. What did Gould expect? That the ghost would welcome them with open arms, eager for a free therapy session? *Thanks, guys, for showing up and reminding me it's time to move on!* It was all so naive. Dr. Gould's team had no idea what they might be up against. They were used to dealing with harmless, confused specters. But Joe sensed the hatred in the club, the desperation and rage that radiated off the walls and dug itself deep into his flesh like psychic fishhooks.

Joe stepped up to the long bar that ran along one side of the dance floor. Moonlight filtered through a skylight, creating a parade of flickering shadows. Normally the shelves would be lined with bottles of liquor, but they stood empty now.

Too damn bad, I could use a drink.

A sudden, ear-splitting sound tore through the space and made him nearly drop his flashlight. It wasn't the scream of a tortured soul but the nerve-wracking noise of audio feedback emanating from a nearby DJ booth. The lights on the mixing table flashed wildly.

Here we go, Joe thought as Tony rushed toward the booth and pulled the plug. The jarring sounds died down.

A tense beat passed as they all traded glances. The temperature dropped and their breath crystallized in the ice-cold air.

It's on.

"You guys feel that?" Nick asked.

Dr. Gould nodded and produced an infrared thermometer. She held it up and eyed the readings.

"Make a note. Temperature is now—"

Gould was interrupted by a heavy wooden door slamming shut with a devastating bang. One by one, their flashlights went dark. The tense breathing of Gould's team was drowned out by another banging sound in the darkness, followed by heavy footsteps.

"Jesus, what was that?" Tony asked.

She's here, dumbass, Joe thought. He didn't need to be a psychic to know they weren't alone now.

From the corner of his eye, he noticed movement behind the red curtain covering one wall. A second later the curtain billowed out, manipulated by a supernatural force. The animated curtain whipped itself around Dr. Gould, like a lasso, and pulled her to the wall.

Gould's piercing cry reverberated, almost drowning out a series of erratic beeping sounds. The temperature gauge and magnetic reader were going nuts.

The team of parapsychologists were still trying to make sense of what was happening when the spirit launched its second attack. Tony cried out as invisible claws sliced open the back of his coat. Blue-black burn marks streaked across the man's exposed skin. He gasped in pain, his legs giving out and his eyes widening in horror. A supernatural force yanked him off his feet and pulled him toward the ceiling at breakneck speed.

Nick and Steve stood paralyzed, caught in a tableau of terror. Only now did it seem to dawn on them what they were up against.

Tony's panicked screams were abruptly silenced by the sound of breaking bone. A second later, he landed on the dance floor, his arm twisted at an unnatural angle and his features contorted in pain.

Joe fought back his own rising panic as he took stock

of the situation. Dr. Gould was out of commission, cocooned in the red curtain. Tony was unconscious and the other two men cowered in the corners, frozen in place. The hair on the back of Joe's neck stood up and he instinctively sensed a presence lurking above him. He took a deep breath before tilting his head upward, dread welling up inside him as he faced the horror above.

He had steeled himself for the worst, but his imagination paled to the reality. The dead model hung upside-down from the ceiling like a spider. Details of her inhuman appearance jumped out at him: snow-white skin, bloodshot eyes, stringy jet-black hair.

For a moment, Joe couldn't move. Screw trying to help the dead girl. She was going to kill them all.

Starting with him.

The steel chain connecting the dance cage to the ceiling snapped. As the cage hurtled toward him, Joe knew no one would be able to bring him back from the dead this time around.

Someone slammed into Joe's side, pushing him from the path of the onrushing cage.

Joe sucked in a sharp breath.

As the newcomer to the scene jumped smoothly to his feet, Joe caught a first glimpse of his guardian angel. The bearded man wore a long, tattered trench coat over a tieless white shirt. He aimed a green, glowing pistol at the spirit lurking on the ceiling. Did he really believe a firearm could pose any threat to a ghost?

But then again, the weapon didn't resemble any gun Joe had ever seen before, and he'd seen extensive arsenals during his military days.

His rescuer squeezed the trigger, and then this battle between life and death began in earnest.

2

W HO WALKS INTO a haunted house—
sorry, haunted nightclub—without any
way to defend themselves?

Wannabe ghost hunters, that's who. Less than forty-
eight hours had passed since my adventure with the
Horne clan, and here I was going head-to-head with a
crazed ghost. My own fault, really. Instead of taking a
much-needed break after facing Morgal, the demon that
killed my parents, I'd thrown myself into a new case.

At the time, it had seemed like a smart move. Or
perhaps my only move. Quality alone time would
inevitably end with me pickling my liver and crawling
into bed with some barfly who harbored advanced
daddy issues. Better to channel my dark emotions into

something constructive, like kicking some spectral butt and maybe saving a life or two in the process. Anything to get my mind off what happened back at the Horne estate.

I'd expected to find the club deserted except for the murderous spirit trapped inside. Imagine my surprise when I ran into a group of amateurs armed with nothing but good intentions and a bunch of useless gadgets. This wasn't my first run-in with Dr. Gould and her merry band of ghostbusters. How many times had I warned her of the potential dangers? Some folks just refuse to listen.

I made sure the man sprawled on the dance floor was okay before I jumped back to my feet, *Hellseeker* in hand. Forged from the steel of a blessed sword, over a century ago, the magical pistol was my most effective weapon against the forces of darkness. Under normal circumstances I would try to help a lost soul. But this particular ghost was a killer. Someone needed to send her packing, to the afterlife or wherever nasty spooks like her went next.

That someone would have to be me.

There are two worlds, I thought. *The world of the living, and the world of the dead. Sometimes they overlap, and sometimes they COLLIDE.*

Like right now.

Determined to wrap things up quickly, I fired two rounds, the magic-infused bullets streaking toward the ghost on the ceiling. In case it wasn't clear, Newton's laws of gravity do not apply to the restless dead.

One bullet slammed into the spirit's outstretched arm. For a split second, the slug remained visible inside the transparent figure, vibrating at incredible speed. A beat later, the model's arm dematerialized, *Hellseeker* working its ferocious magic. The ghost let out a chilling howl as her body evaporated.

It was a nice trick, if you were dumb enough to fall for it. The ghost was wounded, but not banished. Though this was far from over, at least I had bought myself a momentary breather.

I eyed the downed ghost hunter again. This guy didn't strike me as Dr. Gould's normal flavor of armchair parapsychologist. The lean physique, the hardened look in his eyes—not to mention the scar that ran up his neck —gave the man an edge that the rest of Gould's team sorely lacked. This fella actually looked like he could handle himself in a fight. Just not against an enraged specter.

"You alright?" I asked.

The man stared at me with saucer eyes and nodded. He'd obviously never seen someone pump a round into a ghost. Hey, there's a first time for everything.

Guard up, eyes alert, I swept the club with my magical revolver's sights. *Hellseeker* could destroy a specter, but I would have to hit the head or another vital area. Don't ask me how an immaterial dead person can react as if they still have vital organs. It could have something to do with vestigial memories of being alive, or perhaps the mysterious laws of magic governing *Hellseeker*. Either way, we weren't in the clear yet.

A banshee howl tore through the club, and I clenched my jaw. Sometimes I just hate being right.

I looked up. The dead model, one arm now shorter than the other, stalked the length of the ceiling as if it were a Paris runway. Eyes glowing with rage and hatred, she sprinted past a series of nightclub spotlights with jerky, surreal speed, her form shimmering with each loping step.

I fired mechanically in controlled bursts but my magic-infused bullets missed the zigzagging spirit. A heartbeat later, she launched herself at me from the ceiling, arms extended and a shriek erupting from her distorted lips. The howling fury moved like a panther pouncing on its prey and slammed into me with overwhelming force. The impact knocked me over and I crumpled to the dance floor.

Unleashing another piercing shriek, the phantas-magorical vision straddled me with inhuman strength. What can I say: I have a way with women. A pair of legs that didn't seem to end wrapped around my torso like tentacles, and I came face to face with her sinister presence. Death had both preserved the model's beauty and given it a repulsive quality; every living cell inside me instinctively revolted against her unnatural state.

And then her lips found mine in a hungry kiss, turning my stomach while solidifying the link between us...

The world around me changed in a burst of metaphysical light.

I was still in the club, but it was now filled to capacity. A mass of writhing bodies swirled around us, moving to the pounding hip-hop beat. I glanced down at myself, eyes going wide. I was staring down at a long, lean torso and killer legs wrapped in a miniskirt and knee-high leather boots.

Realization hit me. I was inside the model's head, reliving her last moments before she overdosed at the club.

Turning away from the bar, she fought her way through the bobbing crowd. Her movements became more uncertain and erratic as the drugs kicked in. She kept glancing at her cell and re-reading the fateful text message from a guy named Dean that must've driven the poor girl over the edge: *It's over. I'm sorry, babe.*

Breakup via text message. Talk about class, Dean.

Guys smiled wolfishly at her from the surging throng of dancers, lusty hands reaching for her body. She bounced from one embrace to the next, oblivious of the effect she was having on males of the species. Only one man mattered to her, and he'd just kicked her to the curb.

A violent tremor passed through her body, and blood exploded from her nose. Her trembling arms sought support, legs growing shaky, but suddenly no one wanted to touch her. She was going into convulsions... and she was taking me with her.

"Let go of him now!" a male voice shouted. The wave of clubgoers disappeared in another burst of brilliant spiritual light, putting an end to the model's trip down memory lane. I was once again looking at an empty dance floor. I let out a pain-filled gasp, still reeling from the vision of the dead girl's last moments in this world, and staggered to my feet.

Glancing up, I spotted my reflection in the mirrored wall behind the bar and took a shocked step back. The fellow staring back at me was in bad shape. My eyes resembled bloodshot craters, tainted by the spirit of the deceased model. Along my neck, bluish-black burn marks discolored the flesh where the entity touched my skin. Unhealthy perspiration beaded my haggard features. Reliving the death throes of an overdose victim can work wonders for your complexion.

Skulick's long-ago words slashed through my mind. *Don't ever look a ghost directly in the eyes or allow them to touch you. It can trigger horrific hallucinations or make you relive their final minutes on Earth. It ain't pretty. Most of them didn't check out in their sleep.*

No kidding, buddy.

My magical ring, the *Seal of Solomon*, might protect me from a full-on possession—a nasty little trick both specters and demons have been known to pull—but it couldn't stop a determined ghost from playing mind games. At least now I knew that a broken heart was keeping this suicide case trapped in our world. Not that it changed anything.

I tried to take another step and collapsed, spent from the excruciating effort of breaking free of the ghost's hold on me. This was one of the dangers of being blessed with a sixth sense. It might allow you to chat up the dead, but it also acted as a beacon to them. In a way, I couldn't blame them. Wandering around for all eternity, invisible to most of the world, could transform the best of us into a bunch of clingy stalkers with separation anxiety and anger management issues.

In the end, we all just want to be heard and understood.

I saw the model turn toward the ghost hunter I'd saved from being pancaked by the steel cage. He was the one who shouted, forcing the entity to let go of me. Like myself, this latest addition to Gould's team could interact with ghosts, clearly, and that could mean only one thing—he was a psychic. Poor bastard. That would definitely explain why Gould brought him along on this little expedition into the unknown. The man obviously possessed more guts than smarts. Unarmed, he didn't stand a chance against the model's ferocious spirit.

But his bravery or foolishness, depending on how you wanted to look at it, was drawing the ghost's attention. This distraction gave me the opportunity to fight back.

I catapulted back to my feet, *Hellseeker* ready. My steely gaze cut through the club as I tapped into the bastard part of myself. "Hey, you want to know why Dean dumped your chunky ass?"

The model ghost whirled toward me, rage boiling behind those unfathomable eyes.

"No one likes a fat model!"

The ghost hunters gawked at me as if I'd lost my mind. Maybe I had. After all, I was baiting a homicidal apparition—not the smartest move in the monster-hunting playbook. I felt guilty about stooping so low as to resort to body-shaming, but I didn't see another way. I hoped my taunts would make the dead girl's spirit lose control, which might give me an opening.

The first part of my plan appeared to be working.

Objects inside the club began to shake. The row of spotlights running along the ceiling vibrated and the bar's mirrored wall cracked. The specter's keening moan turned into a primal, shrill scream of unbridled rage.

Hell hath no fury like a woman scorned.

As the ghost advanced with quick strides, I brought up my hands in a defensive stance. Once the ghost was upon me, my fist snapped out in a punch. Under normal circumstances, my hand would merely have passed through the ghost, but I was wearing the *Seal of Solomon*. The magical ring allowed my fist to connect with the ghost's chin as if she were solid. I hate hitting a lady, but I make an exception when she's dead and trying to kill me.

There was a sizzle of spectral energy as the punch landed. The model's head whipped back. I followed up the first punch with a renewed burst of bullets from *Hellseeker*. The projectiles stitched her chest and the ghost shuddered, losing shape and form, skeletal figure growing blurry. The model attempted to launch a final, desperate attack, but it was too late. She emitted a pitiful howl and dispersed into thin air.

It was over. For good this time.

I eyed the spot where the doomed model had vanished. The younger me would have told her to rest in peace, but that wide-eyed kid was a distant memory. Instead, two other words came to mind: Good riddance.

3

I freed Dr. Gould from the heavy curtain and helped her get back to her wobbly feet. If I was hoping to receive some gratitude for my efforts, I was in for a rude awakening. Gould's withering expression didn't feel like a prelude to a warm thank-you hug.

"You cold-blooded bastard. You destroyed that poor lost soul, monster hunter, ruining any chance that she might find peace in the afterlife."

Was this woman for real? Anger rose in me, but I did my best to keep it out of my voice. "That precious lost soul was trying to kill both you and your team."

"Selina Hill was acting out," she said with firebrand conviction. "With a little patience, I believe we could've reached her and made her understand that we were here to help."

"Tell that to the poor couple she murdered, and your assistant whose arm she snapped," I said coolly. "If I hadn't showed up, you'd probably all be dead now."

Dr. Gould stayed mum. I doubted that my words resonated with her, but at least she was letting me talk. "There are souls who need our help so they can embark on that final journey," I explained. "But some are too far gone for words. And that's where I come in." I took a deep breath and felt the psychic's eyes boring into me. He was following our exchange with grave interest.

"You okay?" I asked the man.

"Let's just say seeing dead people doesn't agree with me," he said.

"Good news is you'll never get used to it." I walked over to help him up and asked, "What's your name?"

"Joe Cormac." He shook my hand with a surprisingly firm grip.

I'd met my fair share of natural-born mediums over the last few years, and they all shared an ethereal, otherworldly quality, like they already had one foot in the next world. This guy was different. There was a flicker of fear in this fellow's eyes, which suggested that all this craziness was new to him.

"Use your sixth sense, but be smart about it," I advised him. "This isn't a reality TV show and you're not up against Casper, the friendly ghost. These entities are disturbed individuals with incredible powers, driven by unchecked emotions."

"So I noticed," Cormac said in a sober voice. The psychic had a good head on his shoulders, giving me hope that my words weren't falling on deaf ears. For once. I wish the same could be said for Dr. Gould.

I holstered *Hellseeker*, all too aware of the envious glances I received from some of the ghost hunters. Gould might be a ghost-hugging hippie, but the young men on her team looked like they wouldn't mind some blessed weaponry to go with their scientific gadgets.

"Alright, ladies and gents, as much fun as this ghost hunting business can be, I need to catch up on my beauty sleep," I said. "Just try to stay out of trouble and avoid any psychotic dead people."

With these words, I turned away from Gould's team, my trench coat billowing out dramatically. I like to think I know how to make an entrance and exit. It's the time in between that can be more challenging.

I marched out of the club and found a couple of punks circling my spruced-up, jet-black muscle car. I opened my coat, making sure they noticed the green, glowing pistol holstered to my side. A beat passed and they wisely retreated into a nearby alley, having determined that a joyride in my Equus Bass was not worth the price of admission.

I got into the car and seconds later I was blasting down the street, fighting back a wave of tiredness. I was spent, having pushed my mind and body to the limit over the last few days.

Yawning incessantly, I somehow made my way back to our loft warehouse, located on the industrial outskirts of the cursed city. I barely remembered getting in the elevator and stumbling into the loft. I shouldn't have been surprised to find my wheelchair-bound partner, Skulick, still awake and hunched over his flickering bank of terminals. Slashing streams of data bathed his scarred face a spectral green. His watchful eyes, which rarely missed anything, alighted on me.

"Damn, Raven. Did the ghost give you a hickey?"

I touched the burn marks on my neck where the model's electrical field had reacted with my organic tissue. It would heal up in a few days, but until then made for an unsightly blemish. "Do I detect a note of jealousy in your voice?"

Skulick broke into a grin. "I dated my last ghost a decade ago. Nowadays I like my women to have a heartbeat."

Was Skulick joking or offering up another highlight from his monster-hunting past? Better to not even go there. I decide to take it as a joke and said, "Haha, very funny. I'm way too tired for this conversation. Why don't you go back to chatting up some retiree who believes Bigfoot lives in her basement and let me get some much-needed sleep."

With those words, I lurched past my partner and staggered down the length of our loft until I reached the door leading into my bedroom. The modest room had no windows and felt a bit like a prison cell, but I knew no supernatural creature would ever catch me off guard in there. If any beast should find a way to bypass our defenses, they'd still have to come through the front door if they wanted a crack at me.

Well, unless they were a ghost and could walk through walls.

I crumpled on my unmade bed, still fully dressed. Despite my weariness, sleep didn't overtake me immediately. My thoughts kept wandering back to the events of the last few days. Talk about having your world rattled! I faced the demon who murdered my parents twenty-one years ago, and the man responsible for unleashing it. Horne was gone, but Morgal still ruled the pits of Hell. There was no doubt in my mind that I'd go after the beast again, but dispatching higher-level demons isn't a task undertaken lightly. No matter how formidable *Hellseeker* was against the lower minions of Hell, its bullets had failed to make a serious dent against Morgal.

My mind turned toward Jane Archer, the cop who

helped me escape the fallout of the Horne murders. She had left at least nine messages in the last 24 hours. Jane, smart cookie that she was, knew I'd been in the thick of things back at the Horne estate, but she'd let me go, anyway. Part of me desperately wanted to dial her digits —not to confess, but just to hear her voice. If I let myself have feelings for a woman—especially a brave and independent one like Archer—she'd become an easy target for my paranormal enemies. Casual hookups were okay, but a real relationship was out of the question.

I kept telling myself that even as I reached for the phone.

Man, this was going to be a continuing internal struggle. I closed my eyes and instead grabbed the half-empty bottle of Maker's Mark waiting for me on my nightstand. Booze will put even the most tormented soul to sleep. A few swigs later, the liquor filling my chest with a pleasant warmth, I began to drift off into a dreamless slumber. Sometimes the only sane option was to wash away one's problems with a stiff drink or two.

Encroaching darkness swept images of the lovely detective aside. The less I thought about Archer, the better.

Little did I know that I was about to be drawn into a life-and-death battle for Detective Jane Archer's soul.

4

JOE CORMAC MADE his way through the city, his eyes unfocused as he navigated the swirl of humanity. A torrent of faces, the streets exploding with life and energy, both natural and *unnatural*. As he brushed past a store window, albino-white features pressed against the glass, bloodshot eyes following him. He blocked out the apparition as best as he could.

This is a city filled with ghosts, he thought for the thousandth time since returning from Iraq. Things had been bad in Baghdad, but this was somehow worse. Were other urban centers afflicted by the same problem? Or was there something about his hometown that made it difficult for troubled souls to cross over into the next world? Joe had asked himself the question many times, and he wasn't even close to coming up with an answer.

Two weeks had passed since the incident at the night club. His mind kept cycling back to the mysterious stranger and the glowing weapon that could banish spirits from this plane of existence once and for all. Even though Dr. Gould had tried to assure him he wasn't crazy, words were a poor substitute for direct experience. Or being able to share those experiences with someone who could relate in a deeper way. The hunter had shown him that there were others out there who could see the dead the same way he did. But more importantly, there was at least one person who fought back against the shadows.

Ever since that fateful night, he'd been ignoring Gould's calls, unwilling to risk his life again on some fool's errand. The monster hunter had been right—Dr. Gould didn't understand what she was dealing with here. Perhaps the man could teach him, show him a way to use his abilities for good without getting himself killed in the process.

Joe wanted in. Whatever the monster hunter was doing, he wanted to be part of it. But despite his many requests, Dr. Gould refused to offer up the man's contact information. She didn't even give him a name. Nevertheless, he'd managed to dig up some info on the monster hunter. Mostly urban legend stuff from fringe websites. Various rumors suggested that he worked with a partner in a secret base on the outskirts of the city. Maybe that's why on this day Joe had decided to take a long walk through the rougher neighborhoods encircling the shiny metropolis. He didn't have an address but refused to let that little detail stop him. Even if he didn't find the man he was looking for, Joe figured that stretching his legs would be more constructive than staring at the four walls of his tiny studio apartment while obsessing about the lost souls lining up outside his home.

As he proceeded on his long walk, the neighborhood grew steadily worse. Seedy, condemned buildings and the rusted shells of abandoned cars became more common. At the same time, the incessant wails of the dead grew louder, becoming a chorus of the damned. He slowed his pace as he approached a parking lot. A chain-link fence enclosed the makeshift basketball court where African-American and Hispanic men were playing an intense game. On the other side of the fence, a lone, bony figure watched longingly. Joe took in the bloodless face, the torn Jersey matted with gore. He figured the specter must've been a victim of a recent shooting.

The ghost gave him a brief, forlorn look before passing through the fence and vanishing into thin air. Some spirits sought him out, demanding his attention. Others preferred to remain anonymous and retreated when they sensed his presence, not quite ready to confront the dark reality of their situation. One of the players scored a basket, and his team mates exchanged enthusiastic high fives, oblivious to the dead man.

Joe turned away from the game, resuming his haphazard journey. As he walked past a broken-down motel, its sinister neon sign glimmering in the fading light, his attention turned upward. A distorted figure stood on a ledge, dressed in a suit straight out of an old gangster movie. Despite the twelve stories separating them, he felt the entity's hungry, desperate gaze. Its eyes dug into him a second before the man leapt off the building.

With a violent rush of air, the ghost smashed into the sidewalk right in front of him, and Joe jumped back with a stifled cry. Blood pooled around the suicide's broken form. Some of the dead were doomed to relive their last moments, bound to the place where they died, not even aware that they *were* dead...

God, there are so many.

Shaking from the experience, Joe continued his walk through the urban canyons. Suddenly, the four walls of his tiny apartment seemed preferable to this city of lost souls. Up ahead, a bridge cast a long shadow over a river. Joe warily regarded the dark water, and backed away as a bloated drowning victim emerged. He fled the scene as fast as he could.

But there was no escape from the spirits.

Less than a half an hour later, Joe stumbled upon the skeletal remains of a building that had recently burnt down to the ground. Standing in the blackened rubble, the ghost of a little girl. Dead children were the worst. They always broke his heart. The girl tightly clutched her doll and gave him a shy smile. Without warning, the doll began to bubble and melt.

Joe recoiled as the girl's angelic face followed, transforming into a mass of black burn scars. Seconds later, flames began to devour her tiny form. Giving himself an internal push, Joe hugged the burning girl. *Spectral flames can't hurt me*, he told himself. At least he prayed he was right. As he embraced the spirit, his lips moved, mouthing the most soothing words he could find.

It's okay, sweetheart. You're safe now. It's okay. Just let go.

The burn victim listened in hushed silence, and the fire started to die down. She pulled away from him, and ash flaked off her form, the skin restoring itself as she grew whole again. She smiled at Joe.

Seconds later, she disappeared among the jagged ruins of the building, and he felt the presence of the ghost fade away.

A smile stole across his face. He'd helped at least one lost soul move on today.

His chirping cell phone brought him back down to earth. Dr. Gould was calling him again. Mood bolstered, he decided to pick up this time.

"What do you want? You keep this up I'll have to report you for harassment-" he said.

"I need your gift, Joe," the parapsychologist replied, getting straight down to business. "The world needs you. You can't let fear hold you back."

Gould's words pissed him off. She was right. He was afraid. But for good reason. "How many times do I have to tell you this? I'm done with ghosts."

But if that's true, what had he been doing just now?

"I propose a deal?" Gould said.

"What deal?"

"I know you think that the hunter can be some sort of mentor to you. Personally, I think he's a menace to the spirit world."

Joe shook his head impatiently. "Haven't we been over this before?"

There was a beat of silence before Gould laid it all on the table.

"If you really wish to sit down with this man, I can help you find him. I can even give you his name."

"But it's going to cost me, isn't it?"

Gould's silence spoke volumes.

After a long pause, Joe said, "Fine. What do you want?"

5

Joe Cormac sat in the passenger seat of Dr. Gould's van. Rain pearled on the windshield and ran down the glass in fat rivulets. Outside, milky sunlight outlined the stark folds of the countryside located about an hour's drive from the city. A secluded, imposing structure thrust out of the rain-swathed landscape and buckled under the wind-swept sky. Looming guard towers and high stone walls topped with concertina wire dominated the massive complex. There were no signs of any guards—the prison was long abandoned.

"Welcome to Blackwell Penitentiary," Dr. Gould said dramatically. "Former home to some of the most vile and dangerous murderers and psychopaths to have walked the Earth. Eight months ago, a fire broke out, killing more than a hundred inmates and guards, forcing the state to shut down the place. Blackwell has been abandoned ever since."

Talk about the perfect spot to run into lost souls, Joe mused. No wonder Dr. Gould was chomping at the bit to have him inspect the prison. Had she not learned anything from their encounter at the night club? Did Gould truly believe that even the damned could be saved? Joe didn't share her wide-eyed idealism. The war had taught him that some folks were beyond redemption, whether in this life or the next. "Sounds like a lovely place to visit," he said, his voice heavy with sarcasm. "Why now?"

"The state has decided to refurbish the facility. Budgets are tight and inmate populations are booming. It's cheaper to reopen this place than to build a new prison."

"I see," he said, shaking his head. That was bureaucracy at its finest.

"Some of the workers have reported strange phenomena. Bizarre noises, cold spots, shadowy shapes. I'm curious what you might be able to pick up in there."

If you could see what I see, hear what I hear, I wonder whether you'd still be curious, Joe thought. He kept the words to himself, determined to' follow through with his side of the bargain. This would be their last adventure. He would pull off this final job, and Gould would provide him with the monster hunter's contact information.

The van pulled up to the massive structure. A fine drizzle lashed their faces as they piled out of the vehicle. Once again, Nick and Steve were back for more spooky fun, but Tony had wisely decided to sit this one out. Having a ghost break your arm could turn you off the paranormal for good.

Smart man, Joe thought. *Smarter than me, in any case.*

They walked through the rusting main gate and entered the forsaken structure. The damp air couldn't quite mask the foul odor emanating from the damaged buildings. There was something sick and rotten here, something that shouldn't be disturbed.

Cormac was letting his imagination run wild and get the best of him. Plenty of spooky places in the world weren't haunted, and plenty of nice places were veritable nightmares.

Once inside the gutted prison, they faced three levels of empty holding cells, a landscape of peeling paint and rusting steel. Pale shafts of light stabbed through the barred windows. The walls were blackened and scorched, bearing evidence of the fire. Debris littered the floor, turning the dank hallways into an obstacle course. More than once, they were forced to wiggle their way past twisted steel or piles of burned matresses. Their footsteps echoed eerily in the cavernous structure, doing little to alleviate the oppressive atmosphere of the prison.

Even before the fire, dark feelings of despair defined this place. Violence and negative energy coursed through its steel and stone arteries. Joe could still feel it, even though no one had been detained here for months.

As they advanced, the team's ghost hunting equipment chirped and squeaked, a surreal, almost laughable soundtrack in their oppressive surroundings. Joe's sense of foreboding deepened with each step, the air stirring with hints of sinister emotion. He kept picking up fleeting impressions of rage and pain mixed with unbridled hatred.

It's me...my presence. Whatever has lain dormant here is drawing on my powers.

Something had remained trapped in this structure.

Something evil.

All of a sudden, Joe wanted nothing more than to turn back. The dead model's rage at the night club paled in comparison to the fearsome emotions imprinted into the prison's scorched foundation. He needed to get out of this place. Now.

But if he did that, he might never find the hunter or the answers to his questions. Could he really live the rest of his life surrounded by ghosts but powerless to protect himself?

He followed Dr. Gould and her team into a room at the end of a long hallway. The place turned out to be the prison's execution chamber. A foreboding electric chair dominated the eerie space. It faced a large, shattered window that looked out into a witness room. Human misery had seeped into the very walls, the chamber's dark power undeniable.

"Dr. Frank Engelman, one of the worst serial killers the state has ever seen, was executed here the night the fire broke out," Gould said, her voice echoing eerily.

"Jesus, it's freezing in here," Steve said, breath clouding before him.

"This is the coldest room in the whole prison," Nick explained as he took in the readings of his thermometer. "Even colder than outside."

Joe's eyes were fixed to the electric chair. Something was happening. The air shimmered and rippled. A pair of black eyes appeared on the surface of the electric chair. Seconds later, a mouth rimmed with blood-stained teeth followed. More details snapped into focus as a terrifying figure materialized, body jerking as fifty thousand volts of electricity tore through the specter's writhing form. Joe stifled a cry and recoiled from the sight, gripped by terror. The specter's scream was deafening but judging by the calm expressions on Gould and her assistants' faces, only Joe could hear it.

"Dr. Gould, I have to leave," he said, his voice a raspy whisper.

She flicked him a curious look. "You're picking something up, aren't you?"

Joe struggled to maintain his composure as he said, "You don't want to know."

He was done talking. Without uttering another word, he whirled around and stormed out of the execution chamber. Behind him, Steve said nervously, "Maybe Cormac is right. Maybe we should listen to him..."

Joe picked up his pace until he was practically running down the adjoining cell block. He could make out shadowy shapes now in the corner of his eye, dim outlines of faceless spirits lurking in the holding cells that flanked the hallway. These ghosts were struggling to manifest. He could feel these entities latching on to him, drawn to his psychic powers like moths to a flame.

Behind him, fast approaching footsteps grew louder. Dr. Gould wasn't letting him off the hook that easily. Stubborn woman. He looked up, realizing that in his attempt to get away from the electric chair, he'd stumbled into a vast room. Abandoned carts faced enormous boilers and industrial washers. This immense space must have been the prison's laundry room. The hulking, rusting machines cast grotesquely distorted shadows in the muted daylight that seeped through a series of barred windows. He stood still in this mechanical graveyard, the only sound the constant *drip, drip* of copper-colored water escaping from the pipes overhead.

"Cormac, wait up!" Nick cried, his voice ringing hollowly, an alien sound that didn't belong within these cursed walls. Joe was almost out of the laundry room when one of the washers came to life, the sudden noise jolting in the shadowy space.

Joe froze in place, his pulse throbbing in his ears.

He took a step back from the washer and his blood went cold. A pale, disembodied head hovered inside the drum. The same skeletal death mask from the execution chamber.

Too late... It's too late...

The footsteps behind him had become deafening now, and he spun around. Nick, gasping for breath, appeared before him. "Man, what the hell is going on?"

Before Joe could answer, one of the laundry carts careened toward the door leading out of the laundry room. Stunned, Nick whirled toward the rapidly approaching cart. A split second later, it knocked him against a nearby washer, pinning the man against the rusted metal.

Once again, Joe caught a terrifying glimpse of the spectral face, lips distorted into a hungry snarl. Then Nick's six-foot-two, two-hundred pound frame was sucked into the industrial washer.

There was a spray of red and a series of crunching noises.

Joe stared with horror at Nick's mangled body as Dr. Gould's voice rang through the prison laundry room.

"Cormac, can you hear me?"

Her voice was replaced with a shrill scream. Cormac braced himself against one of the washers, terror holding him in its steely grip. He hadn't felt this scared since he'd faced his first insurgent attack back in Iraq.

We should've listened to the monster hunter...

"Cormac!"

Steve's voice made him spin on his heels. The Dominican ghost hunter was approaching with quick steps, eyes wide. His hand reached out for him only...

To pass through his arm.

For an eternal beat they stared at each other, stunned into frozen silence. And then Joe saw the large, gaping hole in the parapsychologist's stomach.

Oh my God, he's dead... and doesn't even realize it...

Judging by the terrified expression in Steve's face, he'd drawn the same conclusion. Slowly, a black mist oozed from his ears, eyes, and nose and rose into the air like a dark angel of doom. The swirling black cloud hovered for a beat and began to take on a recognizable human shape, the spirit previously glimpsed in the execution chamber and washer now materializing fully. Details grew visible. Cracked and bloodied lips, eyes of pure blackness seething with an unholy fire, a skeletal frame clad in a grey, burned prison uniform.

Joe's breath misted as serial killer Frank Engelman stood before him. Steve's spirit flanked him, the dead scientist's gaze edging toward madness. He let out a shrill cry of shocked dismay as his writhing spirit was absorbed by the entity. For a split second, Joe caught a glimpse of Steve's soul inside Engelman. Like a faded TV signal, he flickered across the serial killer's spectral form, lips frozen in a rictus of a scream.

Engelman tilted his head. Joe followed the spirit's malevolent gaze as more shadows were peeling from the darkness. A parade of the damned, prison uniforms baked into scorched skin. Murderers, rapists and the worst psychopaths to have ever walked this earth. That's what Dr. Gould had called them. The souls of all the inmates who'd perished in the fire.

Joe's heart hammered. He couldn't breathe.

A moment later, the spirit of Frank Engelman was upon him, mere inches between them.

Then the malignant ghost stepped *into* him. For one eternal moment, a surreal rush of violent images flooded Joe's mind, too much for him to absorb.

And then his world turned dark, and he felt nothing at all.

6

The two weeks following the incident at the night club were uneventful. No demons to slay, no ghosts to banish. For most people—the sane ones—this would be a good thing. In my case, it had the opposite effect. I was getting more antsy with each passing day. I had nothing to fill the long hours when the world didn't need saving. Maybe I should get a hobby. Something that didn't involve black magic sorcerers and ancient beings of unstoppable evil. What did normal people do on their days off?

I had allowed our battle against the forces of darkness to define our lives and swallow up everything else. Great way to get things done, poor way to live a life.

Every morning I stepped up to my partner's desk,

inquiring about some possible case. And each day I received the identical terse answer.

"It's quiet out there."

Talk about an understatement.

In a weird way, the lack of occult activity scared me even more. It could only mean the forces of darkness were gathering for something big. The proverbial calm before the storm.

After a week without a single supernatural case or sighting, I began to turn my attention to our vast mystical library. There were a million things to learn about the occult—rituals to familiarize myself with, supernatural lore to internalize. But within a few pages, my mind would wander, unable to maintain my focus on the leather-bound tomes before me and the ancient, horrifying truths contained within their dusty pages.

Face it, Raven, you're a man of action. Leave the book-learnin' to Skulick.

Without my work, I felt useless and adrift. Those feelings had always led me straight to the bottle or the arms of a one-night stand—but even those not-so-healthy habits held no appeal now. In short, my extended period of rest and relaxation was driving me nuts. Who was Mike Raven when he wasn't chasing after some ungodly beast? The answer was sobering: He was some guy who spent way too much time hung over on the couch, watching TV and thinking about detective Jane Archer.

My sour mood even began to wear on Skulick. "You ever of think of getting a hobby, kid? Something to get you out of the house when you're not hunting nightmares?"

I shrugged. "My work is my hobby."

"Last time I checked, a hobby is an activity done in one's leisure time for fun."

"I enjoy hunting demons. In fact, I can't think of anything I rather do right now."

Skulick furrowed his brows, his impatience growing. "Our mission isn't a sprint but a marathon. You keep up this pace, you'll burn yourself out."

"Isn't that the pot calling the kettle black? Maybe you should take your own advice, partner."

"I'm stuck in this goddamn chair. You have options."

A ghost had dropped my partner out of a window less than a year ago. Miraculously Skulick had survived but he would never walk on his own again. Considering our growing list of enemies, it wasn't safe for him to venture outside in a wheelchair. My partner truly had become a prisoner inside our loft. I knew Skulick hated feeling limited and confined. Like myself, he had always lived for the action. Being stuck inside had to be wearing on him—and seeing me with a bad case of cabin fever probably wasn't helping his own mental state.

"Does drinking count as a hobby?" I asked. Okay now I was intentionally being a dumbass—but at least it might make him laugh.

Skulick's lips curled into a grin.

"Only if you're a real man who can hold his liquor."

Nice comeback, buddy, I thought as I smiled back at him.

"Kid, I'm not trying to give you a hard time. I worry about ya, that's all. And I don't want you to make the same mistakes I did. This job—this calling—will chew you up and spit you out if you're not careful."

Skulick had a point and I knew it. But identifying a problem was a lot easier than fixing it.

"How's your love life? Have you thought of giving that detective friend of yours a call?"

Skulick had always liked Archer and felt we would make a good pair. He had no idea that I already managed to bungle it up. I regretted my next words as soon as they came from my lips.

"Remind me again what happened to your fiancée?"

Skulick's face darkened. The woman in question had become a victim of a master vampire almost thirty years ago. The tragedy had turned a rising star in the city's homicide division into one of the most feared monster hunters the forces of darkness had ever had to face.

Why the hell had I brought her up? It's like I couldn't be satisfied until everyone else felt as miserable as I did.

"Sorry, Skulick, that was uncalled for..."

I broke off. Skulick had turned away from me to face his bank of monitors again.

This day was getting off to a great start.

Mercifully, that's when the phone rang. The man on the line was none other than Homicide Detective Rob Benson, my liaison at the department. He only called on me and Skulick when a weird case presented itself that required our expert touch. Judging by his grim tone, he was about to share some bad news.

I cheered up immediately and then felt guilty about it.

"Hello, Raven, how have you been?"

"Busy juggling a few cases," I lied.

"Well I hope you can make a little time and join me at Blackwell Penitentiary. We have a situation out here."

The mention of the prison made my ears perk up. I vaguely recalled the place being shut down about a year ago when a terrible fire broke out. Benson refused to offer any further details, but for the detective to reach out to me, some supernatural mayhem had to be going down.

Within ten minutes of getting off the phone, I was seated behind the wheel of my Equus Baas, on my way to the old prison. As I eased my vehicle into the rainy day, I couldn't help but wonder whether Archer would be at the scene when I arrived.

Man, I *really* needed to get a life.

DARK CLOUDS WERE GATHERING around the ominous prison when I pulled up in my muscle car. A fine drizzle pelted my windshield as I parked next to a few police cruisers. The uniformed officers fronting the facility's entrance immediately recognized my wheels. I could tell by the black looks that greeted me as I got out of my car. There was little love lost between me and the cops under Benson's command. Most didn't know what to make of the bearded, trench-coat wearing stranger who tended to show up when things got weird.

"Lovely weather we're having today," I said as I turned up my collar against the rain. My attempt at sarcasm sure wasn't winning me any more friends. I resigned myself to my outsider status, dropped all attempts at charm, and got down to the business. "Benson wants to see me."

One of the sober-faced officers told me to follow

him, and I obliged. The scar on my chest, which the demon Morgal had marked me with twenty-one years earlier, was itching something fierce as we walked down a cell block teeming with uniformed cops. Dark forces had found a home within the walls of the abandoned penitentiary, no doubt about it. I looked around, hoping to catch a glimpse of Archer.

Get your head on straight, Raven. This is a crime scene. Time to focus on the work ahead.

"Glad you're here, Raven," Benson said as he regarded me with an unreadable look. "Maybe you can make some sense of all this X-Files shit. Come with me."

I tipped my head to the officer who had escorted me to the crime scene and said, "Thanks for the tour, brother," and fell in step with Benson. We walked in silence as the big African-American detective led me into an industrial laundry room. I immediately spotted two shroud-covered bodies sprawled across the floor. For a second I thought I caught a glimpse of shadowy movement among the maze of boilers and washers. Spirits lingered here but their presence was weak. Nothing suggested that those ghosts could materialize and harm the living.

"Can I take a peek?"

Benson nodded. Thankful that I'd skipped breakfast, I crouched down before the first body and pulled the shroud back. Mangled, mummified features locked in the rictus of a scream stared back at me. The man appeared to have been dead for months or even years. I'd seen bodies which had aged at such an accelerated pace before. It normally meant a demon had drained their life force

Or perhaps, in this case, a ghost.

The second body was in even worse shape. Limbs twisted at odd angles, a shriveled-up husk of a man.

"I guess now you know why I called you. By the way, we have a survivor."

I arched an eyebrow. "Oh?"

"She says you guys know each other."

Benson led me to the end of the laundry room. A hunched-over figure sat in the corner. My heart sank. Goddamnit, I'd warned Dr. Gould that something like this could happen. My guess was that the two mummies had been her assistants. Poor fools. Dabbling with the occult is a surefire recipe for disaster.

Her haunted face peered up at me, tears welling in her eyes.

"It's all my fault. You tried to warn me, Raven."

"What happened here?"

"Something attacked us..." She broke off, bit her lips, and added, "It took possession of Joe Cormac."

"You better start from the beginning. What were you doing here in the first place?"

Benson answered for her.

"Apparently this lady and her friends decided to play Ghostbusters in an abandoned prison," he said.

"Any particular reason?" I asked.

"Some of the workers have been complaining about weird shit going on," Benson admitted.

"It all started after we entered the execution chamber," Gould said, having found her voice again. "Joe Cormac began to pick up a presence. Said he had to get out of here. Nick and Steve went after him..."

She paused for a moment, took a deep breath, fighting back tears of grief.

"I caught a brief glimpse of the spirit toward the end. I believe it was the ghost of Frank Engelman."

The name was vaguely familiar, but I couldn't place it.

"Engelman was the serial killer executed on the night the fire broke out," Benson explained.

Now I remembered. My mind snapped back to the chilling string of murders which had terrified the city three years earlier. Engelman was one of the really bad ones, a killer for the ages, the type around which the True Crime genre was built. Thirty victims, each one tortured and horribly disfigured. The press had nicknamed him *"Lucifer's Disciple"* because he marked his victims with demonic sigils. If anyone had ever deserved the death penalty, it was Engelman.

"Engelman's spirit was drawing on Cormac's psychic powers. I think it took possession of his body."

This was bad news. Clearly Engelman's spirit must've used poor Joe Cormac's life force to manifest. People like him were basically walking psychic batteries.

"Who is this Cormac she's talking about?" Benson asked.

"A medium who recently joined her team of ghost hunters."

"And where is this *psychic* now?" Benson didn't bother to hide the skeptical note in his voice.

Dr. Gould began sobbing, still moaning that it was all her fault, and I guessed what had happened. Engelman must've hitched a ride in Cormac's body. Most ghosts were bound to the place where they perished. But a medium could change the rules. Some psychics could channel spirits but normally only for brief moments. A ghost would inevitably drain them, leaving a mummified body behind. Only a rare few could harbor another soul for any length of time. Skulick called these gifted individuals *"Soul Catchers."* Unfortunately, Joe Cormac appeared to be one of them.

I balled my hands into fists and my eye twitched.

Blackwell Penitentiary had been Engelman's prison both in life and in death, but he'd used Cormac to escape.

Tricky bastard.

Thankfully most of the other entities that lingered in the ruins of the prison seemed not to have followed Engelman's example. One monstrous spirit out in the world was bad enough.

It was time for Skulick to look deeper into this freak show. Hopefully, he could dig up something that would help me track and bind Engelman before he did too much harm.

As I pulled away from Gould, I sent my partner a quick message. *Need intel on serial killer Frank Engelman ASAP*, my ominous text read. I had a feeling Skulick would appreciate a chance to get back into the swing of things. I trusted Skulick to take care of the research back at the loft, but I wasn't going to leave until I took a closer look at the room where this spook show had begun. "I want to take look at the execution chamber," I said.

I could tell Benson was dying to bombard me with questions, but he kept them to himself for now. Experience had taught him to let me do my thing first.

He escorted me down a hallway and into a room that felt like a freezer. I shivered and tried to visualize myself on of some hot beach on a tropical island. Mind over matter, right? Unfortunately, my attempt at staving off the cold brought back memories of the Volcano Demon and Fire Goddess Pele and her band of fanatic followers that I had battled on Kona six months earlier.

I circled the ominous death chair. This is where Engelman had exhaled his last mortal breath. Too bad riding the lightning hadn't been the end for the infamous killer. A part of him had remained in this plane of existence, unwilling or unable to move on.

I touched the chair. It was a simple wooden structure, blackened slightly by the fire yet miraculously intact. Its shape was horribly familiar. In some ways, the image of the electric chair was as American as Coke and apple pie. Kneeling before the chair, I noticed a series of glyphs and other symbols etched into its surface. The markings radiated an ancient purpose, and I swiftly took a few shots with my cell phone.

"Any idea what it could mean?" Benson inquired.

I shook my head. One thing was for certain— these additions weren't industry standard nor were they the work of squatters. If anyone, Skulick might be able to decipher some of these occult markings.

"We've come across similar occult symbols all over the prison," Benson said. He leaned closer and added, "Are you going to tell me what the hell's going on here?"

"There are ghosts in this prison. Most of these spirits

are the echoes of the inmates who died here, weak and unable to affect the world of the living. But you throw a psychic into the mix and a determined spirit might find a way to feed off his abilities and take possession of his body."

Benson stared at me for a long moment. "So you're saying Engelman is out there."

"It appears that way. Now we need to figure out what an infamous and very dead serial killer might be after."

"I can answer that. The bastard is out for revenge."

"What are you talking about?"

The detective scratched his jaw. "I bet Engelman is going after the person who put him in that chair in the first place."

I suddenly had a bad feeling about where this conversation was headed.

Even though I'd already guessed the answer, I had to ask. "And who would that be?"

"Detective Jane Archer."

7

B lood roared in my ears as I slipped behind the wheel of my ride and mashed the gas, the engine roaring to life. I white-knuckled the steering wheel, my reality reduced to one objective—I had to reach Archer before Engelman did. All my attempts to contact the detective by phone had failed. There might be plenty of reasons why she wasn't answering my calls. Perhaps she'd left her cell phone in a gym locker while she went for a quick workout. Maybe she was at the movie theater catching a flick with a good friend. Or, the most likely explanation, she hated my guts and never wanted to talk with me again.

I refused to entertain the sinister possibility that Engelman might've already gotten to her. At least I tried to refuse, but I was failing miserably.

Over and over, my mind's eye offered up visions of Archer as a mummified corpse. The image made me groan inwardly. I reached up to rub my temple, and the Equus's wheels screeched as I momentarily lost control of the vehicle. I was driving at least thirty miles above the speed limit. At this rate, it was just a matter of time before I would find myself in some high-speed chase with the police. Getting arrested wouldn't help Archer in any way. I told myself to stay calm, hoping logic would win over the mad panic I was experiencing.

Even though my mental pep talk failed to turn off the rush of nightmarish images in my mind, I managed to ease my foot off the gas and the needle on the speedometer began to tick downward. I switched on the radio and prayed some grinding hard rock would prove distracting. The right combo of Queen and AC/DC worked its calming magic, and I somehow reached the city without being stopped or veering off the road. Traffic grew denser as I fought my way through busy downtown streets.

An hour had passed by the time I finally arrived at Archer's prewar apartment building. The three-story walk-up stood on a quiet, semi-private side street lined with trees. Miraculously, I found a parking spot. Dark clouds were gathering in anticipation of an imminent downpour.

As I ran toward Archer's building, a few stray drops pelting my face, an elderly lady walking her beagle emerged and gave me a long, suspicious look. The expression on my face probably didn't exactly inspire much confidence. I caught the door before it could fully swing shut and entered the building. A creepy, dimly-lit hallway awaited me. My eyes zeroed in on a winding staircase flanked by an ancient, poorly maintained elevator.

I let out a sigh of relief as I surged up the stairs toward the third floor. So far, my scar wasn't setting off any alarm bells. There didn't appear to be anything amiss in the building, and I kept my fingers crossed. God knows I hadn't done anything to deserve a break, but Archer was one of the good guys.

My mood darkened when Archer's apartment door jumped into view and neither the cheesy carpet nor the walls in dire need of a new paint job were to blame. Being here brought back the memories of the night we'd spent together—and the regret I'd felt after slipping out of her place at the crack of dawn. Hey, I got scared, so sue me. Losing your parents at an early age can lead to attachment issues. In the end, I'm only human. Nevertheless, returning to the *scene of the crime* was a reminder that I'd blown a potentially great thing and that I deserved every dirty look I'd gotten from Archer since. It also made me feel a bit like some pathetic stalker who couldn't let go. What was I going to tell Archer if indeed she was home? She already suspected I might be crazy, so warning her that she was in danger from the ghost of a psycho killer was probably not going to go over well.

Archer wasn't a novice when it came to supernatural cases. Most cops in the cursed city had encountered the forces of darkness in one form or another since the Crimson Circle weakened the barrier between our world and the world of darkness beyond. Still, coming to Archer with the story of Engelman's return might be misconstrued as some weak, creepy attempt on my part to get back into her good graces. Or, even worse, as a misguided attempt to get into her pants.

All these thoughts were rushing through my mind when the door to Archer's unit suddenly swung open and a muscle-bound hunk emerged from her place. For a beat, my mind went blank. I knew Archer wasn't some nun pining for that one magical night we'd spent together. A woman like her had a million options. I was just surprised she'd go for the macho meathead type. The man studied me for a beat, initial curiosity turning to suspicion. The situation turned even more embarrassing a beat later when Archer's voice cut through the hallway.

"Raven, what the hell are you doing here?"

Hercules Junior arched his eyebrows and turned to the door, where Archer was standing with one hand on her hip and a surprised expression on her face. "Jane, you know this guy?"

At least he hadn't called her *honey* or *baby.*

"Raven, is a special consultant at the force," Archer said. "But that doesn't explain why he's here now."

I shrugged my shoulders and managed a sheepish smile. "I know this looks weird, but I've been trying to reach you for the last hour." With a glance at Muscle Boy, I added, "I guess you've been, uh, busy."

"Why should I pick up your calls when you ignore everyone of mine?" Archer had a point. She'd been trying to get ahold of me ever since the massacre at the Horne estate, but I'd steadfastly ignored all her attempts at contacting me. Partially because I didn't want to relive Morgal's rampage, but also because I was still processing what had gone down that night.

"Listen, I'm here for a reason," I said, my voice bristling with urgency. "There was an incident at Blackwell Penitentiary."

Archer stiffened at the mention of the old prison.

"What happened?"

I scratched my beard, not quite sure how to bring up the topic of ghosts with Archer's special friend hulking over me. She must've picked up on my hesitation because she shot her friend a quick look.

"Charlie, Raven and I'll have to talk in private."

He frowned at her, still not quite sure what to make of me. "Cop stuff," Archer added to emphasize her point.

"Alright, no problem, you know how to find me if you need me."

With these words, Charlie turned away from us. Five doors down, he entered one of the other units. The door had barely snapped shut when the words tumbled from my lips. "Who is that guy?"

"My neighbor. What's it to you?"

How friendly was Archer with her neighbor? I sort of doubted he'd just stopped over to borrow some sugar. And why should I care? I gave myself an internal push to focus on the real reason that had brought me back here.

"What happened at Blackwell?" Archer asked.

Before I could offer anything resembling an explanation, the lights in the hallway flickered. There was a series of pops as, one by one, the bulbs blew out, drenching the corridor in near darkness.

I swallowed hard. Could have been a coincidence, but in my line of work, you stop believing in the random nature of events. The phrase *everything happens for a reason* sort of becomes a guiding mantra when battling demons and supernatural beasts.

My scar started to itch, too. If I needed more confirmation that something weird was up, I had just received it.

My hand reached for *Hellseeker* as the air at the end of the long hallway shimmered, charged with bursts of paranormal energy. A black silhouette peeled from the darkness. It slid across the floor, shifting and bulging, rising up to six feet.

A human shape lurched toward us. A shadow come alive.

There was no sign of Joe Carmac so Engelman must have abandoned the psychic's body for now.

"What's happening?" Archer wanted to know, her eyes wide with growing terror.

"Engelman is here," I said and drew my blessed pistol. As soon as I uttered the undead fiend's name, the entity unleashed a bellowing shriek and rushed toward us at breakneck speed.

8

J udging by the confused expression on Archer's face, she still couldn't see the incoming killer ghost. A small mercy, all things considered.

Engelman moved in jerky jump cuts, his bony features changing with each step, turning into the faces of other men. They looked nothing alike—some bald and others wild-haired, some tattooed, some with biker beards and others clean-shaven—but all oozed an air of raw violence and desperation.

My gut told me these had to be some of the other Blackwell inmates. Mass murderers. Rapists. The grotesque, terrifying faces of some of the most evil men to have walked this earth. Psychopaths and predators, their souls merged with Engelman's spirit somehow. A few seemed vaguely familiar, like I might've read about them in the news at some point or seen their ugly mugs staring back at me from a true crime documentary.

Not every spirit had escaped from Blackwell by hitching a ride inside the psychic. But Engelman had managed to bring along a small army. And all those souls appeared to be under his command.

Great.

"Raven, what the hell is going on?" Archer's voice was shaky, picking up on my fear. She knew I didn't scare easily. Her panicky voice brought me back to reality, breaking the unholy spell Engelman's spectral freak parade had cast over me.

I brought up *Hellseeker* and unleashed a volley at the fast-approaching ghost army. Bullets streaked down the corridor and tore into Engelman. He roared with pain but kept coming at me. The sanctified lead was unable to stop him, only slow him down.

Apparently, *Hellseeker* was no match for Engelman and his legion of the damned. Why was the blessed weapon failing me? Only one explanation came to mind: Engelman had fused with the others ghosts, becoming more powerful than a single spirit in the process.

Powerful enough to overcome my magical weapon.

"Oh my God!" Archer shrank back against the wall. Judging by the sudden terror in her voice, Engelman must've shifted into the visible spectrum, probably triggered by *Hellseeker*'s bullets peppering his spectral form.

Without thinking, I snatched Archer's hand and pulled her toward the elevator. She yanked her arm away from me, glaring, not used to playing the role of the damsel. Glock drawn, she unloaded into the specter, but her bullets passed through the ghost, pockmarking the walls behind the entity. Screams and muffled voices grew audible from the other apartments. No doubt the helpful citizens were already dialing 911.

Hellseeker was almost as useless as Archer's ordinary Glock. Nevertheless, I pumped another round into the incoming ghost for good measure, and Engelman let out an inhuman roar. It seemed that even the dead experienced pain. The souls of the other inmates trapped within the mega-spirit screamed out in unison and momentarily lost coherence, breaking apart. For a split second, I spotted two familiar faces among the dead inmates—the writhing souls of Dr. Gould's two dead assistants. Their cadaverous, haunted faces suggested they hadn't voluntarily joined Engelman's supernatural chain gang. Engelman's spirit had bound their souls to his own when he murdered them at the prison, absorbing them somehow.

Soul Catcher!

In this case, the term applied equally to Joe Cormac

and the super-entity I was sighting down. What was I up against here?

The answer would have to wait as the entities reconstituted themselves, shaking off the effects of *Hellseeker's* bullets.

I kept squeezing off more shots, struggling to keep my growing terror in check. Engelman and the entities whirling and undulating within him recoiled, his form bending and twisting under the impact of each blessed bullet. The continuous barrage seemed to do the trick. There was a final beat as Engelman's midnight-sun gaze bore into us before *Hellseeker* erased the fiend from reality. Engelman was gone...but who knew for how long though? My itching scar was a clear indicator that his evil remained. He and his undead minions were still around, lingering in the air. Weakened but waiting. Biding their time to strike again.

There were innocent people in this building. I might have been a cowardly jerk when it came to women, but I did my best to protect those who couldn't fight back against the forces of darkness. I needed to draw Engelman away from this place. "Let's get out of here!"

For a change, Archer didn't fight me on my latest suggestion. As we rushed down the staircase, she fell in step with me. For a moment, it felt like the old days again, before our working partnership had given way to our growing attraction. Even though some crazed killer spirit was on our tails, a strange sense of happiness gripped me. It was good to have Archer on my side.

Somehow we made it down the stairs and out of Archer's building without another run-in with murderous ghosts. It had started raining and I blinked the drops away. My eyes locked on my wheels. Magical wards protected the Equus Bass and should keep Engelman and his dark horde at bay. At least I hoped it would. The spirits were far more powerful than the ones I was used to dealing with. My hand closed around the handle of the passenger door, and I whisked a still-stunned Archer into my vehicle. As soon as the door slammed shut, our spectral pursuer made his move.

Materializing from thin air, Engelman reached out for me with lightning speed. Bony fingers penetrated my chest like a scalpel and...

The world changed around me in a flash.

I was back inside the oppressive walls of Blackwell Penitentiary, now flanked by a priest and a phalanx of prison guards who whisked me down winding, austere corridors. Unlike the last time I'd seen the prison, there were no signs of the fire. Understanding hit me. I was inside Engelman, walking the green mile and reliving the moments leading up to his execution.

The guards dragged me into the execution chamber.

All too soon, flames would consume the room—and the witnesses who'd gathered behind the observation window. I wanted to warn them, but history couldn't be rewritten. This was a vision of the past, and all I could do was bear witness. I felt myself being brusquely shoved into the chair. Leather straps fastened around my limbs with a taut sense of finality, and an icy metal plate was pressed down on my cleanly shaven scalp. Even though part of me knew this was just an illusion, a memory triggered by the spirit's assault, my heart still raced.

"Do you have any last words?"

I caught a glimpse of my reflection in the observation window. Except it wasn't my face, of course. It was Engelman. And he was addressing the crowd who had come to see him die.

"I was set up. I never killed anyone. I didn't do it! I'm innocent..."

It was the favorite refrain of so many murderers who were about to meet their maker.

But there was something almost convincing about Engelman's words.

Could this monster be telling the truth?

I didn't get much longer to ponder the question. The time had come to die.

When the fifty thousand volts of electricity hit, the

pain was beyond anything I had ever endured. It felt like an invisible hand had cracked open my ribcage and was squeezing my burning heart. Through a haze of agony, I saw the various glyphs light up on the electric chair, turning a fiery red.

The electricity is powering and activating the magical symbols, I thought.

A scream exploded from my lips, and reality returned to normal. I was back in the present day, back in my own body. My face, gaunt and haggard but still undeniably *me*—was reflected in the Equus' passenger window, surreally superimposed over Archer's terror-stricken features as she stared at me.

"Get the hell out of me!" I roared, swinging my fists wildly at the apparition. Engelman reared away from me, a howl of frustration rending the air as his ghostly form vanished once more. The protective power of the *Seal of Solomon*, which I wore on my right hand, must've kicked in and driven his spirit out of my body.

There was no time to celebrate. No time to catch my breath. Driven by pure will, I opened the driver's side door of the Equus and slipped behind the wheel, a shivering, broken mess. Not a moment too soon, either. Engelman's terrifying death mask flickered in my rear-view mirror, features shifting and transmogrifying into the other prisoners. The one-man horde launched itself at the car but bounced off the windshield with a sizzle of mystical energy, the wards working their magic. I had no idea if they'd hold up to a continued assault, and I didn't intend on sticking around long enough to find out.

I fired up the Equus, punched the gas, and allowed the stone arteries of the cursed city to whisk us away.

9

Zipping through rainy traffic, all I could think of was putting some distance between us and Engelman.

The traffic light ahead turned red, and I was forced to slow down. I kept seeing the killer ghosts among the pedestrians crossing the busy intersection. The renewed downpour had transformed their bobbing umbrellas and black raincoats into shadowy, ghostlike shapes, and I gripped the steering wheel a little harder.

I became acutely aware of Archer's presence next to me. I inhaled her perfume, vanilla and soft woods, mild yet adventurous. Just the way I remembered. I stole a glance at her. Rain had pasted her long hair to her scalp, making her look like a pissed off cat that had just been introduced to a bucket of water.

She was still beautiful.

"Are you okay?" I asked.

"Hanging in there," she said, voice shaky. "It's not every day that you find out that a ghost is trying to kill you."

Archer wasn't a novice when it came to the paranormal; after all, we had worked together on a series of strange cases in the past. Nevertheless, investigating a supernatural mystery was a hell of a lot different than directly becoming the target for the forces of darkness.

Engelman's final words haunted me. *I didn't do it...*

There was a reason why his spirit had allowed me to relive the last moments of his execution. He wanted me to know that he'd been set up for the murders. Or at least that he *thought* he'd been set up. Could a ghost lie? Was he trying to throw me off? Or was he truly professing his innocence?

It didn't add up. The two dead parapsychologists back at Blackwell Penitentiary were clearly his handiwork. Even if he'd been innocent once, Engelman had proved himself capable of murder now. My brand of justice had nothing to do with the earthly variety. It was my job to send his vengeful spirit back to hell.

"How can Engelman be back from the dead?" Archer's question pulled me out of my thoughts.

"Skulick and I are still working on the answer to that

one. There was something strange about the prison fire. Somehow Engelman and the spirits of the other inmates remained in this world."

"So why now? Why come after me a year later? And shouldn't he be, you know, bound to the place he died?"

Archer had clearly internalized some of the basic laws governing specters. But someone had thrown out the rule book this time around.

"That's how it works normally, but Engelman found a way around the rules," I said. I quickly told her about Joe Cormac and how the killer ghost must've hitched a ride in the talented psychic.

Archer paused, processing my words, trying to wrap her head around the idea of a "soul catcher."

"So if I understand you correctly, Engelman and the other spirits feed off this psychic."

I nodded grimly. "In a matter of speaking. That's probably why Engelman isn't chasing after us right now. Joe has become Engelman's anchor in this world—he haunts the man the way other spirits haunt places. The ghost can leave the host body for short periods of time, as we just witnessed, but I figure Engelman needs to remain close to Joe Cormac to operate in the outside world."

Archer's mind churned behind her intense gaze. That's one of the things I admired most about her. Sure, she was gorgeous—but she was also sharp as a knife's edge and a brilliant, fearless cop. Beyond wanting to protect her, I was glad to have Archer on my side right now. Although I was trying to sound like I knew what I was talking about, Engelman was unlike anything I'd ever faced.

"Why didn't your magical bullets finish him?"

Good question. I'd been asking myself the same ever since I pumped an entire magazine into Engelman and the undead bastard had kept on coming at us.

"I'm not sure. Somehow Engelman's spirit has fused with the other Blackwell inmates, strengthening him." I was reminded of the strange occult symbols etched in the electric chair. Had Engelman turned his own execution into a hellish ritual of some kind, one that had triggered the fire and trapped the souls of all the inmates? I hoped Skulick's big brain was closer to coming up with an explanation for this craziness.

Archer chewed on her bottom lip and then said, "So basically I'm up against the ghosts of some of the worst criminals this city has ever seen. Just another day on the job, huh?"

I knew Archer was using humor to mask her fear but at least she was trying to maintain a positive attitude. I kept my voice calm as possible as I spoke. "You're not alone in this, Archer. None of these entities will get a chance to get close to you again. Skulick and I will make sure of that. We'll stop Engelman and send the ghosts straight to Hell where they belong."

I tried to sound more confident than I felt, and must've succeeded to a degree because some of the tension eased from Archer's shoulders. She didn't quite smile at me, but her mouth relaxed into something that was almost like her usual sassy smirk.

The traffic lights changed, and we were moving again. Fortunately early afternoon traffic was light, and we were making good progress.

"Where are we headed now?" Archer wanted to know.

"I'm taking you back to our headquarters."

Archer shot me a look and cocked an eyebrow.

"Headquarters? I'm finally being allowed inside the secret clubhouse?" Despite having worked on a few cases, our base of operation had always been off limits. I'd made the mistake of letting someone in once—just once—and it had nearly killed Skulick and resulted in the deaths of a dozen people.

I shook the memory of Celeste Horne away.

"Don't worry. My base of operation is magically protected by wards. Not even ghosts can get past our mystical defenses. You'll be safe with Skulick."

There was a flicker of something soft—gratitude,

maybe, or vulnerability—in Archer's lovely features. It was quickly replaced by an expression of steely resolve. "What are you saying? You're expecting me to sit this one out? In case you forgot, I'm the one who put Engelman behind bars the first time around. I can handle myself."

I was expecting Archer to protest, but I had to try. She wasn't the type to sit out a fight and follow the action from the sidelines.

"I know you can kick butt with the best of them. But we're talking about ghosts here. Ghosts that even my weapons aren't able to stop."

"Right, which is why you need backup in the field. What are you going to do?"

Good question. I'd been wondering about that one myself.

"The psychic is the key. Without him, Engelman can't survive beyond the walls of Blackwell Penitentiary. We find Joe, we find Engelman."

Archer mulled this over. "And what are you going to do when you find him?"

"I'll cross that bridge when I get to it."

I wasn't being completely forthright with Archer. I did have the first seeds of a plan. Maybe there was a way to sever the link between the psychic host and the supernatural parasite that had attached itself to him.

But if I was wrong, if Engelman couldn't be safely contained without harming Joe...well, I would do what needed to be done to protect this city.

To protect Archer.

I made a sharp left, intent on merging onto the freeway and heading back to the loft warehouse Skulick and I called home.

"Tell me more about Engelman and how you caught him," I said. "Benson gave me a basic rundown, but you would know the case better than him. Engelman was a pretty nasty character even when he was alive, right?"

"That is putting it mildly. They didn't call him 'Lucifer's Disciple' for nothing."

Archer's face seemed to grow a shade paler as she mentally dredged up the ghoulish details of the case. I felt like an ass for making her relive it, but there was no way around it.

"Why the nickname?"

Archer sighed. "Engelman was a history professor specializing in comparative religion, mythology and the occult. During his off hours he was moonlighting as a full blown Satanist.'

Okay, not exactly the most well-adjusted hobby.

Archer continued with her profile of the fiend. "The bastard would carve sigils into his victims, a way of promising their souls to the demons he worshipped. These weren't just murders but sacrifices designed to earn him favor of the Prince of Darkness himself. The sick bastard said that he was trying to earn a reward for his *handiwork*."

I perked up. "What kind of reward?"

"Based on the information in the diaries we found at Engelman's house when we arrested him, he was hoping Hell would turn him into a demon of some sort. Or at least give him supernatural abilities. The guy was insane." She paused, glancing at me, her eyes wide and questioning. "Wasn't he?"

A chill traveled up my spine. Engelman's mad motivation echoed Desmond Horne's infernal goal. My years of battling dark forces had shown me that power-crazed warlocks and occultists could be even more dangerous than supernatural creatures. After all, mortals had a hell of a lot more to prove.

For a moment, a dark sense of melancholy washed over me. Would this madness ever end? For every monster Skulick and I put an end to, three more seemed to take its place. My eyes met Archer's. I wanted to tell her that everything was going to be okay, despite what we had seen tonight. But I couldn't lie to her.

"How did you catch Engelman?" I asked, dodging her question.

Archer's stare grew distant as she continued.

"At first his victims seemed random but my partner and I eventually managed to find a common thread which connected three of his victims. They'd all attended various classes and seminars given by Engelman."

As I let Archer's words sink in, one detail jumped out.

"You mentioned a partner. Who were you working with when you caught Engelman?"

Alarm edged into Archer's expression as she realized where this line of questioning was headed. "Ballard. Detective Lucas Ballard. I think you met him a few times."

"Where's Detective Ballard now?"

"He's stationed uptown nowadays. Do you think..?"

Her face filled with a dark realization. "Engelman is going to go after him."

If he hasn't done so already, I thought grimly.

"Both you and Ballard put him in that chair. He doesn't strike me like the type who forgives or forgets." My attempt to sound glib about the whole thing failed miserably.

"We have to warn him," Archer said.

I nodded. It sounded like Skulick and I might be getting two visitors today. "I'll find Ballard and bring him in. But first I'm taking you to headquarters. You'll be safe—"

Archer's withering glare cut off my words.

"You'll do no such thing, Raven. We're going to get Ballard first before we do anything else!"

God, she could be stubborn. Didn't she realize she'd become a target for an army of dead psychopaths. My stomach twisted into a knot at the thought of something happening to Archer. Almost as If she had read my thoughts, she grabbed my arm. I looked down, halfway expecting sparks to pop where her fingers touched my skin.

"I know why you've been avoiding me, Raven. I've got your number. You think if we get too close, if you let me in, the ghouls and goblins might start coming after me. Newsflash: I'm a cop. Every day I go to work could me my last. But that's who I am. That's who I'm always going to be." She smiled sardonically. "And apparently I ended up a target anyway."

Archer's logic was hard to argue with. Plus it was becoming increasingly difficult to think with her this close to me.

Resigned to the fact that arguing with her was a pointless exercise, I sharply spun the wheel. Tires kicked up plumes of rain water as I performed a sharp U-turn seconds before reaching the freeway ramp. My maneuver earned me a wail of angry honks and shouts from the other drivers. As Archer reached for her phone, I floored the gas.

We were headed uptown. I prayed we would reach Ballard in time.

FOR A DISORIENTED BEAT, Joe had no idea where he was. Or *who* he was for that matter. Every part of his body ached, and he could barely move in the cramped space where he found himself. A glance upward revealed that his right hand had been handcuffed to a heavy object of some kind, limiting his movements and making escape impossible. He pulled on the cuff, and metal painfully cut into his skin.

As his eyes slowly adjusted to the gloom, he began to recognize his prison. He was inside the back of Dr. Gould's van. A thin trickle of light shafted through the windshield and illuminated the ghost hunting equipment.

Why was he in the van? Where was Dr. Gould?

Further investigation revealed that the handcuff was attached to the steel frame of one of the car seats. Again he pulled on the cuff, and a jolt of biting pain traveled up his arm and set his rotator cuff on fire. Cursing under his breath, he licked parched lips, suddenly aware of how thirsty he was. And his stomach was growling too. How long had he been out? And what had happened back at Blackwell Penitentiary?

Without warning, the image of Engelman's death mask features flashed before his eyes, and he remembered with terrifying clarity how the spirit had turned his mind inside out, transforming him into the host for so many dark souls. They'd taken possession of his body, locked him up inside his own mind while they used him to navigate the world of the living. Their souls had all touched during his possession, turning his world black. Fragments of these spectral monsters survived inside him even now, psychic splinters in his soul. By sharing their broken, twisted minds, he felt as though he'd experienced their crimes, their sick desires and dark deeds.

And at the heart of the violent storm, Engelman's cry for vengeance had burned bright. But below the hatred and rage, there had been something else.

He'd heard a plea for help, a desire to communicate a grave injustice that had been perpetrated against him. But why would Engelman see himself as a victim? How could a monster like him demand justice of any kind?

It made no sense.

Before Joe could fall further down that rabbit hole,

the air in the van crackled with an ominous sense of power. Reality warped and sizzled. A beat later, Engelman's albino skull-mask peeled from the van's metal ceiling.

The ghost had returned.

And that could mean only one thing. Once more Joe would serve as the human vessel for these lost spirits.

"*No.*"

Engelman's spectral features remained locked in icy indifference while his ghost form undulated, expanding around Joe like a dark cloud. Ectoplasmic tendrils of black energy entered Joe's body through his mouth, nostrils, and ears. Breathing became impossible as the darkness enveloped his entire being, drowning out all other thoughts.

Joe wouldn't remember uncuffing himself.

He wouldn't remember climbing in the front of the van and starting the engine.

Wouldn't remember pulling into traffic, speeding on his way to his next target.

Soon, vengeance would be his.

10

The echoing boom of gunshots filled the indoor firing range of the uptown precinct, and the biting smell of cordite hung heavily in the air. Gingerly, Archer and I made our way toward the source of the commotion. The thick-muscled, six-foot-three figure fronting the red line had seemingly declared war against the row of silhouette targets. The report was deafening as the shooter emptied his magazine in three-shot rhythms. Two in the chest, one in the head. Over and over again. A lethal machine.

If the cursed city had more cops like Detective Lucas Ballard, the forces of darkness might have picked another city to invade.

After a final deafening barrage, the shooting paused.

Ballard cracked his neck, stretched and shifted from one foot to the next. He lowered his firearm and slammed in a fresh a magazine.

Looks like someone is ready for round two.

We were almost upon him when he finally took note of our presence. Recognition flickered over his steely blue eyes, framed by safety glasses, as Ballard turned toward us. His mask of focused professionalism gave way to a warm, welcoming smile. Suddenly, the detective seemed a lot less intimidating despite the still smoking gun in his hand. He slipped off his protective goggles and engulfed Archer in a bear-hug.

"Talk about a nice surprise, Jane. How have you been?"

"Same old, same old. The psychos and scumbags are keeping me busy."

Not to mention the creatures of the night, I thought but kept silent.

Ballard grinned, which made him look like a little kid on steroids.

"You guys downtown dealing with as much weird shit as we do up here?" Ballard's full attention shifted to me as he offered his hand. "What's up, Raven? Hot on the tail of the ghoul of the week?"

I managed a thin smile. As usual, my reputation

preceded me. Based on the few times our paths had crossed in the past, Ballard knew all too well of the type of cases that required my involvement. Bad news followed me around like a shadow.

"Hi, Ballard. You're looking good. Been hitting those weights?"

"Just trying to keep up with the bad guys, you know."

As if to make a point, he cross-drew with lightning swiftness, and one of the targets grew a third eye.

"I gotta stay prepared," Ballard exclaimed. "This city has gone to hell in a handbasket. You know that better than anyone, Raven." He paused, frowning at me. "Come to think of it, all this freaky nastiness kicked in after you showed up on the scene."

Here we go again.

Ballard wasn't the first cop to draw a correlation between me and the horrors which terrorized this city. By now I should be used to the accusations—or at least thick-skinned enough to let them roll off my shoulder. But it hurts when people think you're the cause of a problem which you spend day and night trying to fix.

It hurt even more because it was true to a degree.

Skulick and I had failed to stop the Crimson Circle three years ago from completing their terrible master plan. Even though we interrupted their spell, the ritual succeeded in weakening the barriers between worlds, and the city became the new frontline in the war between light and dark. It's why Skulick and I had set up shop here to be in the heart of the action, where we were most needed.

"So what made you drop by today, Jane?" Ballard said, eying his old partner curiously. "If Raven is tagging along, it sure isn't a social call."

She hesitated before answering. "We believe someone out there might mean to harm you."

Ballard furrowed his brows quizzically. "What are you talking about?"

"I don't know if you've been following the news," Archer said, slowly working her way up to the weirdness. "There's been an incident at Blackwell..."

An electric jolt passed through my scar, and I bit back a cry. Over the years I've gotten used to the sharp pangs of pain signaling incoming danger. It was a small price to pay for an advance-warning system which had saved my skin on multiple occasions. That said, normally there was a build-up to the discomfort but this time around was different. It felt like someone had doused my chest with gasoline and lit it on fire. I gasped and gnashed my teeth.

We weren't alone anymore.

Noticing my struggle to maintain a manly façade in

the face of nerve-shredding agony, Archer trailed off and her hand went for her gun.

Ballard stared at us both, confused by the sudden change in our moods. "What's going on?"

"He's here, isn't he?" Archer said.

Ballard shot her questioning look. "Who's here? What's happening?"

"Frank Engelman has returned from the grave." Archer said, her voice a glassy whisper. Ballard was still wrapping his head around this answer when Engelman made his move. One of the bullet-riddled targets in the far back of the range warped and distended with super-natural energy as it came to surreal life. The first living target silhouette was quickly joined by others, the moving images now leaping down the range like an army of shadows come to life. Somehow Engelman was animating them—they'd become an extension of his will.

Ballard was still staring open-mouthed at the rapidly advancing horde when I drew *Hellseeker*. I squeezed off a few shots, striking the first of the living targets. The impact knocked the two-dimensional silhouettes down. Encouraged by my success, Archer decided to join the party, her bullets felling the other targets as effectively as *Hellseeker*. Paranormal energy might be animating the targets, but they weren't supernatural creatures in their own right the way vampires, demons or ghosts were.

One of the targets popped up right in front of Ballard, light streaming through the bullet holes he'd put there moments earlier. The target's head arced toward him like a guillotine, opening a deep gash in his arm. Blood sprayed as Ballard staggered back with a cry. Relentless, the animated target leaped at Ballard...

BLAM! The barrel of Archer's pistol found the animated target and blew it away.

Nice work.

Archer flashed me a triumphant look, her lips curled in a wild grin, face flush with adrenaline.

Don't get cocky, babe.

I scanned the room for Engelman. The dead serial killer was undoubtedly the invisible puppeteer pulling the strings here, but he remained invisible even to my sixth sense.

Archer's victorious smile might have been a tad premature. The downed target silhouettes bounced back to their feet, their forms now sporting brand new bullet holes.

Not good. Not good at all. Time to make a quick exit.

"Come," I urged Archer and Ballard. He fell almost reluctantly in step with us. His pain-filled gaze wandered from Archer to me, scarlet soaking his shirt where the target had slashed him. He looked pale, his face sunken in with terror. The faraway expression in his face was one I'd seen many times before. What was supposed to be another day at the office for the detective had turned into a waking nightmare. Working an occult case wasn't quite the same as going head to head with a murderous ghost.

Hellseeker leveled, I knocked open the door at the end of the target range, expecting Engelman to pop up in front of me. I let out a sigh of relief when the corridor ahead appeared deserted. I took a deep breath and led the way. The plan was simple. Get Ballard and Archer out of the precinct, into my ward-protected car, and then to headquarters while I figured out what our next move should be. The detectives would be safe while Skulick and I figured out the best way to deal with Engelman. Good plan in theory, but my churning gut told me the dead serial killer might have a few more surprises in store for us.

Sometimes I really hate my job.

Two uniformed officers appeared around a bend in the hallway, both men on their way to the range. I was so on edge that I nearly shot them, which I'm guessing would not have gone over well with the good people of the cursed city PD. They were talking animatedly to each other, unaware of the threat posed by a pissed-off ghost—or a paranoid monster hunter.

Without warning, two pairs of skeletal hands morphed from the walls next to them. The clawed limbs reached for the stunned officers, spectral energy penetrating living flesh. A heartbeat later, two entities fully peeled from the walls and stepped into the bodies of the shocked officers. As the ghosts vanished inside the cops, sickly sclera consumed both pupil and iris, turning their eyes a blank, milky white. Now under the command of the spectral body snatchers, the men immediately drew their firearms.

"Get down!" I yelled. My warning came almost too late as bullets whizzed overhead and chopped the walls of the corridor. Archer recovered first. She returned fire but made sure to target the officer's legs. The men went down without a sound. Seconds later, I was upon them. Maybe the men could still be saved. They were innocents, merely in the wrong place at the wrong time.

I turned the bodies over. Staring back at me were two mummified corpses that bore zero resemblance to the two officers. Only the black police uniforms holding the shriveled remains served as a reminder who they'd been in life. The attacking ghosts had burned up their life force within seconds. White hot rage bubbled up inside of me as I spun around, seeking the cruel engineer behind this latest horror.

"Show yourself, you fucking bastard!" I yelled. My challenge was met with an eerie silence. Apparently Engelman wasn't willing to reveal himself–at least not yet. Seeing my anger mirrored in Archer's expression helped me regain my sense of control. I couldn't allow emotions to rule me.

Calm down. Breathe. Stick to the plan. And get the hell out of this place. Now!

My inner mantra seemed to do the trick.

"Go!" I said.

The force in my voice snapped Archer and Ballard out of their paralysis. Seconds later, we were running down the hallway again. There were no further surprises as we reached the end of hallway, burst through another door, and entered the underground parking structure that housed the precinct's patrol cars. Blue-and-white cruisers sat parked in rows on both sides of us. My eyes found the Equus Bass parked ten cars down, a massive, jet-black outlier.

We'd made it.

Almost.

As we navigated the gauntlet of cruisers, an engine roared to life, followed by the sound of burning rubber. For a moment, I almost expected to catch a glimpse of

Engelman or one of the other inmates screaming toward us in one of the police cruisers. Instead, I saw a green van barreling toward us at full speed. I immediately recognized the vehicle. I had last encountered it parked outside of Club Link—Dr. Gould's Mystery Machine. Behind the wheel was none other than Joe Cormac, just the man I wanted to see.

He drove like a man possessed—mostly because he *was* possessed. His eyes glimmered with a dark fire. Skeletal faces shimmered and flickered over his own features, X-ray like glimpses of the spirits dwelling within him. How many passengers had hitched a ride inside the medium?

The answer was way too many, if his physical state was any indicator. I got a good look at him as he drove toward us. His features wrinkled and wizened, his formerly black hair now almost snow white. The spirits were devouring his life force, draining him like a battery. The mummified corpses of the dead parapsychologists came to mind. Engelman and his spirit army had sucked them dry. The same was now happening to Joe Cormac, albeit at a far slower rate.

All these thoughts raced through my mind in mere seconds and then the van was upon me, a steel beast hell-bent on wrapping yours truly around its fender.

At this moment, I desperately wished I was a wizard

of some sort and could just magically make my car come to life and whisk us away in the nick of time. But the Equus Bass remained where I had parked it earlier. We would have to fight our way to my car.

"Aim for the tires!" I screamed.

A second later, both Archer and Ballard, who had finally regained some of his cool, unleashed a hot volley of lead. Tires shredded, and the van spun out of control, barreling past us. The deafening sound of rending metal filled the parking structure as it crashed.

I kept advancing toward my car. Gun up, ready for another vehicular attack. Nothing happened.

Instead, Joe kicked the door of the van open and staggered outside. Blood caked his hair, and his eyes were wild and feral. For a beat he regarded me with a blank expression before tendrils of spectral energy shot from his wide open mouth. One by one, spectral entities materialized. It was high time to get out of here.

Moving fast, we made it to the Equus, got inside my vehicle and tore out of the garage, barely avoiding a collision with a police cruiser pulling into the structure.

I wanted to warn the poor bastard, but there was no time. The cursed city's finest would have to clean up this mess. Right now, the most important thing was getting Archer and Ballard to safety.

And me, too, I guess. Given the number of times I'd ruined Engelman's day, I had probably made his hit list.

"Is this, like, a normal day in your line of work?" Ballard asked in the back seat. He looked a shade paler than when I first met him.

You don't know the half of it, buddy, I thought as I mashed the gas, the Equus' engine howling as we tore down the street.

Welcome to my world.

11

L ightning speared the night, bathing our headquarters in a sickly glow. Ballard faced Archer, Skulick, and myself, his features locked in a haunted mask—a shadow of the former hotshot I met hours earlier in the target range.

Some people could handle the supernatural. Others fell to pieces.

My gaze flicked to Archer. This was the first time I had allowed her access to our base of operations. I knew she was studying the place, her eyes scanning the walls lined with occult tomes, mystical texts, and exotic relics. I'd imagined bringing her here before, granting her access to the inner sanctum, but Skulick and Ballard were definitely not part of the fantasy. "Nice bachelor pad, guys, but it could use a woman's touch," she said. "A plant or two would work wonders."

"Very funny."

After duking it out two months earlier with a swamp creature brought to life by an occultist dabbling in elemental magic, I could happily go through life without ever looking at anything green again, but Archer didn't have to know that.

"I'd offer you the full tour, but…" I trailed off with a shrug.

To my surprise, Skulick wasn't giving me too much heartache over my decision to bring her to our loft. Unlike Celeste Horne, Archer had proven herself to be a trustworthy ally over the last year. Judging by the way he kept stealing glances at the two of us, he was trying to get a sense of our relationship status. Skulick and I shared pretty much everything—he was like a father, older brother, and partner all rolled in one. I would take advice from him any day of the week, but I wanted him to stay out of my love life. Or lack thereof.

I turned my focus back to Ballard, who nervously was cracking his knuckles. The man was clearly out of his element and still deeply shaken from his paranormal experience.

"What are we doing here again?" Ballard asked.

"At this moment in time, our base of operation is the

safest place in the city," I said with as much patience as I could manage. "No ghost can get into this structure undetected."

"That's not quite true," Skulick interjected. "You remember that time when the Ratcatcher breached our defenses..."

I shot Skulick a dark look, silencing him. No need dredging up past exploits. Ballard looked nervous enough as it was. "There is always an exception to the rule. Rest assured, Engelman and his merry band of criminal psycho-ghouls would have a hard time overcoming our security measures."

Ballard shook his head and rubbed his face, almost as if he was hoping to wake from the nightmare his life had turned into. "This is nuts! How can Engelman be back from the dead? We fried his ass."

"I can only imagine how hard this must be," I said. "But you saw what happened back at the target range with your own eyes. Engelman won't stop until he gets his revenge."

"What about the spirits of the other inmates?" Archer asked. "Why did all their souls remain behind? And how is Engelman controlling them?"

"Excellent questions" Skulick said. "Any theories, kid?"

Sometimes I think Skulick still sees me as the sidekick in this operation, the Robin to his Batman. I responded with zero hesitation.

"The markings on the chair make it pretty clear that Engelman turned his execution into a ritual of some kind."

"What sort of ritual?" Archer wanted to know.

"That's the million-dollar question, isn't it?" Skulick said.

Judging by the self-satisfied grin on my partner's face, he had already put some of the pieces together and was letting us play catch up.

I eased closer to Skulick's giant desk, which was littered with empty coffee cups. My partner had been burning the midnight oil on this one. A collection of monitors revealed the photographs I'd taken with my phone at Blackwell Penitentiary. There was a wide angle shot of the execution chamber, two creepy images of the electric chair, and a series of close-ups of the occult glyphs etched into the wood.

"So what have you been able to dig up?" I asked.

"There was a survivor that night."

My eyebrows ticked upward.

"I managed to track down Dirk Shellback, a former prison guard," Skulick explained. "He is currently retired on a disability pension. Our phone chat proved to be quite educational."

Skulick tapped a button on his cellphone and replayed their conversation.

"Strange things had been happening at Blackwell ever since Engelman arrived." The voice had a scratchy quality to it, like each word was a struggle to get out. I got the sense Shellback was old and ailing but also determined to tell his story. *"What do you mean?"* Skulick asked in the recording.

"We were the guards and he was the prisoner, but we all knew what the score was. Engelman was running the show."

There was a pause before Shellback continued.

"Things were changing at Blackwell, and Engelman was responsible. The warden knew something was up. He even tried to stop the execution."

"Why?"

"He thought that if Engelman died in that chair, something terrible would happen."

So much for the idea that Engelman might be innocent.

Skulick cut off the recording. "He got that right. I studied the photographs you took at the prison, Raven. Engelman turned Blackwell Penitentiary into a giant lightning rod for psychokinetic energy."

"English, please, for those of us who didn't binge watch *Stranger Things*," Archer said.

Skulick pursed his lips and then made another go at

an explanation. "Engelman magically transformed the electric chair into a power source for an occult ritual designed to bind him to this plane of existence even after his death."

"Talk about holding a grudge," I said, hoping to cut the tension in the loft, but no one laughed. Tough crowd.

"My guess is that the wiring in the old prison couldn't handle the ritual's sudden power surge. A fire broke out. Hundreds of inmates died. The ritual was designed to stop Engelman's soul from crossing over, but instead…"

"It ended up trapping the souls of hundreds of other inmates on our plane of reality," Archer finished. I smiled at her, absurdly proud of how well she was dealing with the situation.

"His soul must've fused with their spirits, strengthening it immeasurably, which would explain why *Hellseeker* can't seem to damage them permanently," Skulick said.

I pondered this. "Is there a way to reverse the ritual?"

Skulick knit his brow in concentration. "The electric chair appears to be the key." He zoomed in on the creepy image I had snapped of the execution chamber. "The chair acts as an anchor to our world. All the energy flowed through it when Moreau initiated this ritual."

My eyes narrowed. I finally understood where Skulick was headed with this. "What are you saying? You destroy the chair, you send Engelman and rest of his ghouls packing?"

"That's my guess. But the glyphs protect the chair. I suspect that's why it didn't get damaged in the fire."

I frowned. "Is there a way to reverse the chair's protective magic?"

"That's what I'm looking into."

If anyone could do it, Skulick was the man to crack this mystical puzzle.

"Did you find anything else?" I asked, sensing that Skulick was still not quite done.

"Something about the state of the two dead parapsychologists caught my attention."

Skulick punched up crime scene pics of Dr. Gould's mummified assistants.

Ballard let out a disgusted groan. "Jesus Christ!"

"Those are the bodies found at Blackwell?" Archer asked.

I nodded grimly. "Dr. Gould's assistants."

The mummified remains of the two murdered parapsychologists seemed to glare back at us, almost as if demanding justice for what had happened to them. Their deaths were a sharp reminder of what I was fighting for.

"What the hell happened to them?" Ballard asked.

I didn't try to hide my anger as I spoke. "Engelman sucked them dry. He fed on their life force, and he'll do the same to you if he gets the chance."

Ballard shook his head. "This keeps getting crazier and crazier!"

I couldn't agree more. But that didn't mean it wasn't happening.

Welcome to my life.

My partner called up another series of crime pictures, and a new set of dead bodies flickered on-screen. These skeletal, mummified remains looked almost identical to the first set. Only the background was different. Both bodies had been found deep in the woods, judging by the thick undergrowth and trees surrounding the mummified remains.

"What are we looking at?" I asked.

"The first body was discovered about five months ago, the second was reported seven weeks before the most recent incident. Both corpses were found in the forest surrounding the penitentiary. The high levels of lead on the remains match the forensics on the two most recent killings as well as the tox readings taken at the prison."

I mulled this over, weighing the implications. There

had been other victims. Earlier victims. And they both had visited Blackwell Penitentiary.

Still trying to wrap my head around this latest revelation, I said, "Let me get this straight. Assuming Engelman tried to possess these people, how did they end up outside the prison?"

"I believe someone dumped the bodies," Skulick said.

"Were they identified?" Archer asked.

Skulick pensively massaged his scar which ran along his cheek. "Yes, and that's where things get really interesting."

New images appeared. A man in his late thirties, and a young woman who had to be college age. Attractive, happy, alive. A far cry from the skeletal mummies on-screen.

"Meet Rob Sinclair and Sarah Harris, two of the most respected mediums in the psychic community."

This latest revelation took my breath away. "Engelman must've tried to hitch ride in them too."

"It appears that way," Skulick said. "Not every medium is a soul catcher. It takes a rare breed of psychic to hold so many souls for any length of time and not burn out in the process."

Skulcik's words reminded me of Cormac's deteriorating state. There were limits even for a soul catcher.

"How do you think these other psychics ended up at Blackwell in the first place?" I said.

Skulick shrugged. "The location has been a hotspot for parapsychological research pretty much from the start. They could've been random ghost hunters."

"But then their bodies would still be in the prison, wouldn't they? But it almost looks like someone dumped these psychics *after* Engelman sucked them dry. Someone who didn't want people to know what had happened."

"My thoughts exactly," Skulick said. "It's almost as if someone was bringing psychics to Blackwell in the hopes that Engelman could successfully attach his spirit to them."

"Who would want to do such a thing?" Archer asked.

"Perhaps the same person who brought Cormac to Blackwell prison?"

Skulick had phrased it as a question, but his eyes met mine with a terrible certainty. One of us had to say it out loud.

I took a deep breath and then gave voice to a dark possibility. "You think Dr. Gould had something to do with this." Skulick's silence was all the answer I needed.

"I made some phone calls in the ghost hunting community. Word is Dr. Gould worked with both of these psychics before they went missing."

Ballard frowned, mirroring my own confusion. "Why would a parapsychologist want to help the spirit of a serial killer?"

Skulick's answer was to tap another button on his keyboard. A new picture appeared on-screen. It showed Engelman with a group of young people.

"This picture was taken a month before Engelman's arrest three years ago. The students were doctoral candidates studying mythology and the occult."

My eyes narrowed and fixed on the person standing closest to Engelman. Her hair was different, worn loose instead of in a tight bun, but her green, catlike eyes framed by round glasses were unmistakable. Staring back at us was none other than Dr. Gould.

12

"Dr. Gould knew Engelman while he was alive."

Skulick's words landed with the force of a punch to the gut. Dr. Gould had known Engelman; in fact, she'd been a student of his. I'd believed Engelman's escape to be a random event facilitated by Dr. Gould's foolishness, but what if it was more than that? The parapsychologist had struck me as a harmless but misguided idealist, someone who wanted to do good. A former Goth girl drawn to the dark side who had turned her former hobby into an adult obsession. I'd tried to warn her a few times about the danger she was putting herself and her team in, and she'd seemed sane at the time. But now I wasn't so certain.

Had she specifically recruited these psychics, hoping

that one of them might turn out to be a soul catcher? Was she a secret accomplice who'd helped Engelman's spirit escape?

In a strange way it almost made sense—except for one glaring detail. Why had she been left behind at Blackwell when Engelman's spirit took over Cormac's body? Gould was the one who'd called in the murders of her assistants, and her shock when I questioned her had felt genuine. What game was she playing here?

"I believe Gould helped Engelman," Skulick said, cutting through my wildly churning thoughts. "The question is why."

"Perhaps she was more than just a student," I said.

"You think Gould and Engelman might've been an item?" Archer asked.

Skulick nodded slowly. "It might explain her dedication, and why she would go to such lengths to help his ghost."

The possibility of a relationship between Gould and Engelman raised other question. Had Gould known what Engelman was up to before his arrest? Had she helped him with the arcane ritual? Worse, had she been his willing accomplice all along? I bit back my rising anger. I hate being played for a fool.

"This is nuts!" Ballard said. "Ghosts and magic and zombies."

"Nobody ever said zombies," I protested lamely.

Ballard shook his head. "Why don't we haul Gould in for questioning?"

"Ballard," I said. "That's a good idea."

If Gould and Engelman had been involved romantically, she might know where he was now or what he had planned.

"Skulick, you figure out how we can destroy the electric chair and send Engelman and his freak parade to the deepest pits of Hell." I eyed Archer and Ballard. "I'm heading out to have a little chat with Dr. Gould."

Archer held up a hand. "Hold on a sec. What are we supposed to do while you play detective?"

"*Play detective?*" Was someone trying to hurt my feelings?

Archer pointedly ignored my question and said, "If some crazy ghost is after us, I'm not just going to sit around while you risk your life. We're coming with you, Raven!"

Ballard seemed about to protest, clearly not thrilled by the idea of facing the supernatural again, but Archer's glare stopped him cold.

"And how am I supposed to protect you from Engelman? We barely got away the last time. You're safe here. I can't worry about you while trying to crack this case."

Archer sighed with frustration. "I'm going to go out of my mind trapped in this place with nothing to do."

"Look around. We have a great occult library. Skulick won't mind if you check out a book or two."

My partner glowered at me but said nothing. He can be a bit territorial about our collection.

"I don't need to be reading ghost stories when I'm living in one, thanks."

"Well there is always my DVD collection. You ever see *The Hangover*?"

Ballard perked up. "Dude, I love that movie!"

My gaze landed on my partner. "Skulick, you won't mind the company, right?"

"The more the merrier," my partner said dryly while staring daggers at me. Great, now everyone in the room was mad at me. My work here was done.

Before Archer could take drastic measures like handcuffing herself to me, I was out the door and on my way to Dr. Gould's apartment.

13

The irregular outline of Gould's gothic five-story apartment building cut a forbidding silhouette. The main entrance was open, and I easily slipped inside. To my surprise, I didn't bump into a living soul as I made my way upstairs. I had a growing sense that the building was abandoned. The place felt, for lack of a better word, *dead*. Ghosts had a way of getting under one's skin, even for a guy in my line of work.

I'd made a few phone calls on my way to Gould's place. The parapsychologist hadn't shown up for a university class she was teaching, and no one had heard from her since the Blackwell incident. That was under-standable enough, considering what had happened, but I still had a bad feeling about her disappearing act.

I never understood why some women were drawn to evil men, especially killers. Charles Manson, Jeffrey Dahmer, Ted Bundy—all had more than their fair share of female admirers. Some women might perceive a serial killer as the ultimate bad boy. They probably thought all these psychos needed was the love of a good woman. It was like the plot of a bad romance novel come to life. I'd seen enough women fall prey to weres and vamps over the years to know these stories never had a happy ending.

I reached Gould's apartment and rang her doorbell. When there was no response, I knocked for good measure. Leaning against the door, I listened for any signs that someone might be home, but a yawning silence greeted me. Unwilling to just give up, I quickly picked the lock. I had no scruples breaking the law under the right circumstances, and I felt the current situation more than qualified. Still, I was glad Archer was tucked away safely at the loft. I doubted she would approve.

Less than a minute later, the lock gave way with an audible snap, and the door cracked open. A dark apartment awaited me. I entered, *Hellseeker* drawn and muscles coiled, ready to explode into action if the situation should call for it. Trickles of light seeped into the place through half-drawn blinds. As I moved deeper into the unit, my eyes adjusted to the gloom. Dr. Gould's predilection for the paranormal was evident everywhere —occult tomes and esoteric artworks covered every square inch of the place. There were books on witch-craft, ESP, ghosts, and demonology. Skulick would have felt right at home.

I passed a small desk littered with papers. Scanning its contents, I discovered more damning evidence against the parapsychologist. There was a Google map print-out of Archer's apartment and an address unfa-miliar to me but which had to be Ballard's residence. I leafed through multiple shots of the two police precincts where the detectives were stationed. I was beginning to understand how Engelman had managed to track down his quarry so quickly. Gould had done all the legwork while he remained trapped at Blackwell. She had researched the targets, learned about their habits, and fed the information to the dead killer.

Talk about a deadly duo. Bonnie & Clyde eat your hearts out.

As I rifled through the stack of papers, I spotted Dr. Gould's laptop. I powered it on, but not surprisingly, the device was password protected. The police department's cyber-crime unit would have no problem breaking through the security…except for the whole pesky break-ing-and-entering thing. I'd strolled in here without a warrant or backup, so legally nothing I found could be used in a court of law.

A sudden sound made my heart jump into my throat, and I spun around. Best I could tell it had come from the closed door at the other end of the living room.

My grip tightening around *Hellseeker*, I advanced toward the door. I held my breath, but no other sounds disturbed the perfect silence.

Upon reaching the door, I clenched my jaw and pushed it open. It was a bathroom. There were candles everywhere, many of which had burned down to noth-ing. The flickering flames of those that remained lit painted warm shadows in the small, white space. There was something almost romantic about the scene if your idea of romance included an ornamental, crimson coated dagger with a handle shaped like a skull. Someone had dropped the blade on the tile floor. I suddenly knew what would be waiting for me behind the closed shower curtain, but there was no turning back at this point.

Steeling myself, I pulled the curtain back in one swift motion and came face to face with Gould's naked corpse. I fought back a ripple of revulsion. Lifeless eyes peered back at me. Deep gashes on the parapsychologist's wrists left no doubt as to how she'd perished. Even more disturbing were the strange glyphs drawn in blood on the bathtub walls. I'd seen these symbols before. They were identical to the ones etched into the electric chair back at Blackwell Penitentiary.

Leaning closer, I took note of the framed photograph resting on Dr. Gould's chest. It showed her and Engelman together, looking at each other the way only lovers can. The two of them had been a couple, no doubt about it. I scooped up the frame, hoping to take a closer look. The moment I moved the photograph, my mind went blank. The frame had covered up a final magical symbol etched in blood across Gould's snow white chest.

It was the mark of a demon, a sigil of summoning.

I gasped, a shiver exploding up my spine. I knew this symbol, would recognize it anywhere. It was identical to the one my last client had been marked with.

This was the sigil of Morgal, the same demon who'd killed my parents.

For a moment, I stood frozen, my mind having gone blank. As the shock wore off, my brain began to put the pieces together. All spells or rituals require a supernatural power source. The bigger the spell, the more energy was needed. Human sacrifice to a demon was just about the strongest mojo possible. This was serious magic.

"What are you doing here?"

The harsh voice behind me jerked me out of my thought process, and I spun around. Outlined in the doorframe was the nude, bloody body of Dr. Gould. My gaze ticked from the corpse in the tub to its preternatural twin looming in the bathroom's doorframe.

I was looking at Gould's ghost. Had to be. There was no other explanation. The irony shook me to the core. Here was a woman who had dedicated her life to studying the paranormal and now her spirit had become one of the restless dead, trapped in the world of the living.

Worst of all, she had chosen this horrific fate for herself. Did the presence before me know what had happened to her, or was she confused about her own state, unsure whether she was alive or dead? Keeping my fear in check, I decided to find out.

"Dr. Gould?"

At the mention of her name, the ghost turned away from me, almost as if the sound of my voice had made her lose interest. Instead, she walked back into the adjoining living room, blood raining down her wrists, marking the beige rug with a red trail.

"Why did you do it?"

No answer was forthcoming. She stepped up to the

window, and her form seemed to lose substance, merging with the light spilling in from outside.

"He doesn't love me anymore," she said, her voice tinged with a palpable sadness. "Maybe he never did. Maybe it was all in my head. Or maybe the ritual changed him. All that matters to him now is revenge..."

I let her words sink in. Love had motivated Gould's actions. Somehow, she must've believed that a reunion would be possible with her dead lover. Unfortunately, once she finally provided him with a host body that could hold his spirit, he'd cast her aside, driven by an undying need to go after Archer and Ballard. Her love scorned, she had opted for suicide. Had she foolishly believed their spirits would be reunited? My answers would have to wait. At the moment, there was only one question that mattered.

"Where is Engelman now?"

"I don't know." Suddenly her voice grew confused. "Who are you? What are you doing here? What do you want from me?"

The candles in the bathroom flickered violently.

I stood my ground as a gust of wind whipped through the apartment. Gould's spirit wouldn't be at peace until someone reversed the ritual that bound her spirit to the place of her death.

It wouldn't be me.

The parapsychologists had lured innocents to their doom. She'd crossed the line. She wouldn't be receiving any help from me.

Almost as if Gould had read my thoughts, she shouted, *"Get out!"*

I happily obliged.

14

I left Gould's apartment and immediately headed back to headquarters, eager to share what I've learned with Skulick. Archer was impatiently pacing back and forth in the loft when I stepped out of the elevator. Ballard sat in a leather armchair nearby, a couple of books on demonology on his lap and an empty highball glass beside him, looking out of his depth. Someone was getting a *hell* of a crash course on the dark side.

I mentally resolved to cut the poor guy some slack. Both Ballard and Archer were coping with the situation the best they could. Outside, rain tapped the roof like a hive of angry wasps. A little sunshine might've brightened the mood, but the weather refused to cooperate.

Just another beautiful day in the cursed city.

Archer appeared relieved to see me. It seemed there was a first time for everything.

"How did it go?" she asked.

I quickly brought them all up to speed. My partner listened with grave interest as I told him about the role Morgal had played in the ritual. As soon as I finished, Skulick gestured toward his bank of monitors.

"We seem to be on the same page, kid. Check out Engelman's last interview before his execution."

He brought up a video on the monitor. Engelman, clad in an orange prison uniform, sat in a brightly lit room while a reporter fired off a series of increasingly banal questions. I couldn't care less what Engelman planned to have for his last meal before they fried him or how many letters he'd received from lovelorn women. I was far more interested in the crude tattoo poking from the v-neck of his prison shirt.

The mark of Morgal, identical to the one on Dr. Gould's chest. I'd never seen it in any of the other shots of the serial killer—he must've branded himself while behind bars on death row. Like Dr. Gould, Engelman had turned himself into an integral part of an arcane ritual.

"It shouldn't come as a surprise that a professor of comparative mythology and religion would be able to use his esoteric knowledge to his own advantage," Skulick said matter-of-factly.

Something about my partner's words gave me momentary pause. Skulick's understanding of the supernatural was uncanny. What if he should ever be tempted to use his arcane expertise to his own advantage?

The video froze, the mark of Morgal filling the screen. We were up against our old arch nemesis once more. No matter what, it all came back to Morgal.

"What's going on here?" Archer asked, picking up on the unvoiced emotion between us.

"Engelman drew on the power of a demon when he performed the ritual that's keeping his spirit in the world of the living."

Archer searched my face, picking up on the barely contained emotion in my voice. She knew I was holding back a crucial piece of information. Her eyes narrowed as she said, "And you've faced this demon before, haven't you?"

I nodded gravely. A part of me wanted to share the full story with Archer, but this wasn't the place or the time to go into the details of my past. I was thankful that Archer didn't push further.

"So now that you've identified this demon, you boys

will be able to cook up some sort of counter-ritual, right?"

"We're going to focus on the electric chair. The chair survived the fire because it has been touched by Morgal's essence," Skulick explained.

I could see Ballard and Archer's eyes glaze over and I jumped into the conversation. "The proper exorcism ritual should weaken Morgal's link and allow us to physically destroy the electric chair, sending Engelman and his merry band of super psycho-freaks straight to Hell."

"Now we're talking," Ballard said, eyes lighting up. Archer's ex-partner had snuck up on us, his glassy eyes widening with a new sense of hope and purpose. I caught a whiff of Scotch on his breath.

My focus shifted back to Skulick. "Something else has been bothering me since I learned of Morgal's connection to all of this. Why is my scar responding to Engelman's approach? Shouldn't Morgal's magic cancel it out?"

I was thinking of my last case, when my scar failed to detect Morgal's hellhounds. The demon had left the scar on my chest twenty-one years ago when he killed my parents. It responded to the presence of all supernatural beasts—except for Morgal.

"I can only guess." Skulcik scratched his chin thoughtfully. "Perhaps Morgal's evil activated the spell, but the ritual wasn't created by the demon. Take a look at this!"

A new image flashed on-screen. This one showed an aerial view of a dense jungle landscape. Ancient pyramid-like ruins thrust from the thick canopy. "These are ruins of Mayan temples located in Guatemala. From 250 to 900 AD, the Mayan civilization supported one of the densest populations in human history. Then they disappeared in the space of only twenty years. Which raises an important question: What happened to cause this collapse?"

I fought back a twinge of impatience. Skulick was a genius when it came to research, but he wasn't always great at getting to the damned point. Beside me, Archer shuffled her feet and snorted out a quiet breath.

"Just let him do his thing," I whispered. "Trust me, he's going somewhere with this."

A fresh series of images appeared. Skulick had been busy. These new photographs showed close-up views of the various excavated Mayan temple structures. He zoomed in on the ruins, and a set of familiar glyphs jumped into view. My brow turned upward, and I let out a low whistle. The markings bore a striking resemblance to the ones I'd found on the electric chair. "You're saying Engelman resorted to an ancient Mayan ritual to return from the grave?"

"It appears that way," Skulick replied. "This is what we know, based on some of the writings on the temple walls. A bloodthirsty high priest by the name of Totec ran a death cult over a thousand years ago. Think of him as the Mayan equivalent of Rasputin—a scumbag who sacrificed thousands of slaves to the death god *Yum Cimil*. Some of the other priests feared Totec's rule of blood and conspired against him. After numerous failed assassination attempts, one succeeded. But the priests weren't prepared for what happened next. Totec's spirit returned to seek bloody vengeance."

"So both Engelman and this Totec character used the same ritual to cheat the Grim Reaper?" Archer wondered.

"I believe this is where Engelman drew his inspiration," Skulick said. What's more disturbing is what happened next to Mayan culture. Totec transformed thriving urban centers into cities of the dead."

More shots of the various archeological sites flickered across Skulick's computer. Carved images and statues showed a shadowy, skull-faced entity hovering over hundreds of mummified corpses. Attempts by an ancient culture to capture and make sense of the horror.

"The spell not merely bound Totec's spirit to our world but also gave him an appetite for the souls of the living. Remind you of anyone?"

My eyebrows ticked upward. "Are you saying there have been more incidents since Engelman made a go for the uptown precinct?" Archer asked.

A grim-faced Skulick nodded. "I've been getting reports of other attacks. Engelman's been leaving a trail of mummified corpses across the city. The reports are disconcerting, to say the least."

That was an understatement. Things were spinning out of control. Besides having to worry about Engelman gobbling up the souls of the living, I also now had to worry about Gould. She'd used the same Mayan ritual to remain in our world which suggested she too now had the ability to feast on the souls of anyone unfortunate enough to set foot in her place. And if she should somehow find a way of attaching herself to a medium... The thought of having to deal with two soul-eating monsters at the same time sent a chill up my spine. I had to stop Engelman–sooner rather than later.

"This thing is spreading like a virus," I said.

Skulick nodded. "Engelman and his trapped spirits are feeding on the living at a geometric rate."

"Christ, it just keeps getting better!" Ballard said. "How the hell do you guys do this job without going insane?"

This job is what's keeping me sane. At any other time, I would have voiced the flippant response, hiding the truth in a joke, but not today. A cold terror had gripped me. Engelman was like no enemy we'd ever faced before.

A beeping sound whisked me out of my grim thoughts. I swapped a quick glance with my partner. The incessant electronic whine spelled trouble. Someone had tripped one of our sensors.

Skulick immediately punched up our security feed. The bank of monitors came alive with flashing red lights. We used both modern technology and mystical wards designed to keep supernatural enemies from breaching our base.

"What's going on?" a nervous Ballard asked.

"Looks like we have company," Skulick said in a tight voice. A familiar face dominated one of the CCTV feeds. Joe Cormac fronted our warehouse's main garage bay, his dark gaze fixed on the security cam.

The bastard wants us to know he's coming, I realized, deeply unnerved by the cocky expression on the possessed psychic's face. Why was Engelman announcing his approach like this? What game was he playing?

"How did he find us?" Skulick said. I cursed under my breath, and Skulick swiveled toward me, eyes slitted with suspicion, hands clawing the armrests of his wheelchair. "There's something you're not telling me, kid."

I hated it when Skulick treated me like a sidekick, but this time he had a valid reason to be upset with me. I should have come clean from the start.

"Engelman tried to take possession of me earlier today, but the *Seal of Solomon* stopped him."

Skulcik furrowed his brows. "When were you planning on telling me this?"

"It didn't think it was a big deal," I lied.

"In this game, everything is a big deal."

My partner was right.

"You think that's how he found us?"

"It appears Engelman is able to absorb the knowledge of the souls he consumes or even touches."

"How safe are we in here?" Archer said. Skulick's pensive silence didn't inspire confidence.

Outside our warehouse, Engelman stepped closer to the security camera. He was close enough for me to make out his eyes, which swirled with malign energy. And then the eyes cleared, the fiend's brashness replaced with confusion and terror. There was only one explanation for this change in expression—the spirits must've evacuated their host. And that meant...

I whirled and spotted Engelman's eerie form streaking across the large skylight overhead. I whirled and caught more glimpses of the dead inmates beyond the rain-streaked windows. Engelman and his ghost army were surrounding the warehouse.

The wards will hold, I told myself, but suddenly I didn't feel so confident. Engelman wasn't playing by any of the usual arcane rules. Best to steel myself for the worst-case scenario.

Archer and Ballard studied me with growing concern. They couldn't detect the invisible monsters swirling around our warehouse, but they sensed my fear.

"We're in trouble, aren't we?" Archer said.

My answer was to draw *Hellseeker.* I expected the spirits to make a go for the ward-protected windows, but no attack came. Why weren't they even bothering to test our defenses?

My tension grew as the seconds ticked away. Time stretched. Beads of perspiration dripped down my face as I circled the windows, keeping pace with the floating apparitions outside. And then I picked up another sound—an approaching helicopter. I cast a glance outside the window. The searchlights of the rapidly incoming police helicopter speared the night. What the hell was going on?

Meeting my questioning gaze, Skulick switched on the police band. I caught only every second or third word, but it was enough. The law was closing in on our warehouse. Apparently, someone had gotten the crazy idea that I'd murdered a couple of officers at the uptown precinct and taken Detectives Archer and Ballard hostage.

Keeping *Hellseeker* in my right hand, I awkwardly maneuvered my cell phone out of my pocket and dialed Detective Benson. As soon as he picked up, I nearly shouted, "What the hell is all of this, Benson? Why is half the department closing in on my home?"

"Raven, eyewitness accounts place you at the scene when this craziness went down, not to mention the security footage of you taking off with two of our officers. I know you didn't do it, but the commissioner wants you brought in. I think he doesn't like you."

That was putting it mildly. Commissioner O'Connor was devoutly religious and had always been deeply disturbed by my so called pagan methods. Despite an alarming number of weird cases in the city, some people still preferred to live in denial.

"They're going to take you in for questioning, one way or another. You can either cooperate..."

"Benson, this is bullshit," Archer interjected, leaning over to speak into the phone. "We're under attack by—"

The line hissed and crackled and then went dead. Either Benson had hung up—not likely—or else

Engelman didn't want to give us a chance to explain ourselves. Our security system had been designed to keep unwanted intruders at bay, whether dead or alive, but it wasn't a fortress. We couldn't keep the law out if they were determined to breach our base of operation.

I had no doubt Engelman had called the cops and told them where our headquarters were located. He would use the law to gain access to Archer and Ballard. He'd merely have to wait for the cops to enter the warehouse and arrest us. Once we were outside, he and his undead minions would strike. By the time the law realized it was all one big set-up, it would be too late for Archer and Ballard.

And, more likely than not, me. I caught sight of the shadowy shapes positioning themselves on the neighboring rooftops. SWAT sharpshooters.

"Okay, guys, we're getting out of here now!" I declared.

Ballard raked a hand through his hair. "I don't know, man, maybe you should just turn yourself in. We can explain that you didn't actually kidnap us. I mean, you sort of did, but..."

"Shut up, Ballard," Archer said. "Raven, how are we supposed to get out of here?"

A series of police cruisers and officers had taken up position around the warehouse. Trying to barrel through the perimeter in my Equus Bass was tanta-mount to suicide, even for a guy who battled demons and ghouls in a bullet proof, ward-protected muscle car.

A wise man knew when to retreat. "Leave that up to me," I said, trying to sound more confident than I felt. "I have a plan."

15

The engine of my Equus Bass roared to life in the underground parking structure. Archer eyed me nervously, while Ballard looked a tad pale in the backseat. If he barfed on my painstakingly restored vintage upholstery, I was going to kick him out of the car and leave him to Engelman's tender mercies.

"How do you expect to get past those cops outside again?" Archer wanted to know.

"Let's say the main garage bay is not the only way out of this place."

Archer gave me a long look, and I grinned back at her. "Every secret base must have a back door."

With these words, I mashed the gas and twisted the wheel, steering my car straight at the back wall.

Archer looked at me as if I'd lost my mind. Couldn't blame her. I often looked at myself the same way in the mirror.

Impact imminent, I flipped a switch and the wall rumbled open, revealing a second exit. But this one didn't lead to the surface streets. Instead, it led into a tunnel that wound its way deeper underground. Soon, we were blasting down the secret passageway, lit only by the car's headlights.

"This tunnel runs about a third of a mile underground. It lets out near the freeway exit."

Archer flashed me an open-mouthed stare. The network of old underground freight tunnels running below the warehouse district had been one of the main reasons Skulick had selected the area for our base. Originally built to hold telegraph and telephone cables, they were later used to haul freight before being abandoned in the last decade.

Skulick believed in always having a back-up plan, and I silently thanked him for making a point of always being one step ahead of the bad guys. I worried about leaving him behind by himself, but we couldn't all become fugitives from the law. Someone had to stay behind to clear up the situation. Just about now, he would be granting the cops access to our headquarters. I pictured armed SWAT barreling into our place, laser dots flashing across Skulick in his wheelchair. Even with the door open, the magical barrier should hold. Engelman would not be able to enter the facility. But if the cops dragged my partner out of the secure building...

I had given my partner my protective magical ring, the *Seal of Solomon*, which should keep him safe. I told myself that Skulick knew how to handle himself; he'd gotten out of more than one tough scrape over the years. The man had nine lives—I just hoped he hadn't used them all up.

Less than two minutes later, the tunnel tilted upward and the Equus Bass shot into an abandoned mechanic shop located about a half mile from our headquarters. We'd purchased this second property at the same time as the warehouse.

Lowering my windows, I could hear thumping rotor wash echoing through the derelict neighborhood. We had successfully cleared the ring of law enforcement officials surrounding the warehouse. As I barreled out of the empty shop and pulled in the road, Archer shook her head.

"Do I even know you?" she said.

"Never hurts to have a few tricks up your sleeve." I allowed myself a hint of a grin. I rarely saw Archer look impressed.

I pulled onto the nearest freeway exit and shot away from the cursed city like a bat out of hell. We had earned ourselves a brief reprieve, but there was no doubt in my mind that Engelman was going to keep coming after us.

I was done playing defense. It was time to strike back.

JOE CORMAC BLINKED, a man waking from a nightmare. Both his hands were cuffed to the steering wheel of the Hummer they'd stolen after ditching Dr. Gould's van, and his mouth was gagged. The car was currently parked across the street from the monster hunter's base of operation.

The terrible irony of his predicament wasn't lost on Joe. He'd gotten into this mess because of his desire to track down the man whose name he now knew to be Mike Raven. Well, he'd found him—but at what price?

He watched in helpless frustration as Engelman and his ghastly followers encircled the warehouse. Watched as the cops arrived. Watched as the main doors opened and the men swarmed the building, guns and batons raised. None of them looked his way. Even if they had, the vehicle's tinted windows made him invisible to even the most prying gaze. Engelman had chosen his ride carefully.

The thoughts of Engelman and his ghostly band of undead psychos had become his thoughts, their nightmares his own. And he was beginning to understand what Frank Engelman was truly after. God, how he wished he could somehow contact Raven and share with him what he now knew. The threat was far greater than he could imagine. He had to warn the monster hunter before it was too late, but how?

His eyes ticked back and forth inside the vehicle, but restrained the way he was, escape was impossible. Engelman left nothing up to chance. Desperation mounting, he watched as the cops emerged with a man in a wheelchair. This had to be Skulick, Mike Raven's partner—another detail gleaned when Engelman momentarily touched Raven's soul.

The dead man didn't seem to realize that possession was a two-way street. Joe had gotten better at sifting through the dark entity's thoughts, and what he had learned was more terrifying than anything he could have imagined, more evil than anything he'd witnessed in Iraq.

His eyes widened with frustration as Engelman appeared behind the cluster of cops. None of them seemed to be aware of the invisible predator in their midst. None except Raven's partner. Skulick turned and looked right at the ghost. Like his young protégée, the seasoned monster hunter could see the dead. Joe wanted to shout out a warning, but it was too late. To his surprise, there was no fear in the wheelchair-bound man's face as the specter dove toward him, bent on possessing Skulick's mind and body.

For a few seconds, Engelman's phantom form was inside Skulick, ghost and man fused. Skulick began to writhe and contort, and an instant later, the ghost bounced away from him. What had stopped Engelman? Raven's partner had to be using a protective talisman of some sort. Joe wished to God he'd had something like that.

As soon as the explanation occurred to him, Engelman materialized in the passenger seat, his inhuman features horrific to behold. The cuffs snapped open and the gag was removed by invisible fingers. To Joe's surprise, a sense of triumph lit up Engelman's inhuman eyes. The former professor didn't seem to be disappointed about failing to take possession of Skulick.

As Engelman invaded his body once again, their souls momentarily touched, and Joe understood why Engelman was far from being defeated.

I know where Raven is headed next, know what he is up to...

Engelman's thought invaded his soul. He might have failed to take over Skulick, but he had learned some important information.

No one will banish me from this world before I exact my revenge, the guttural voice inside him said.

Engelman's words echoed through his mind for a beat before the lamentations of the damned inmates drowned out all other thoughts.

16

Blackwell Penitentiary sprouted from the stark landscape like a malignant tumor. Thunder exploded as sheets of wind and rain lashed the windshield of my car, and I knew we'd all be soaked the moment we set foot outside.

Worst of all, my partner wasn't answering my calls. Stomach churning with worry, I forced myself to stay focused on the task ahead.

I had a bad feeling about this one.

As I maneuvered the Equus Bass toward the prison's massive, rusting steel entrance, my doubt deepened. I remembered the spirits which lingered and lurked in the shadowy recesses of the penitentiary. Would those weakened spirits turn as soon as they detected our presence?

Engelman had brought along the most fearsome psychopaths on his quest for vengeance, so I hoped the entities that remained within Blackwell's walls were lesser criminals and the innocents who'd gotten caught in Engelman's spell: the warden, prison guards, and other workers who'd perished in the ravenous blaze.

I parked the car right in front of the prison gate and glanced at my two passengers.

"Are you ready?"

Both Archer and Ballard nodded in grim-faced silence. After the spectral encounters of the last few hours, the idea of entering a prison filled with ghosts probably wasn't exactly at the top of their bucket lists.

I pulled up the collar of my trench coat and opened the door. Icy rain pricked my beard and sent shivers down my back. I was ready to brave the horrors waiting for us within the bulwark-like walls of the prison. Or at least I tried to convince myself that I was ready.

Sizzling electricity speared the oily black sky as I popped open the trunk of my car and removed a spare gas can. Soon, the prison would burn again. But this time, the flames would set those poor souls free once and for all. At least I hoped that's what would happen.

Armed with the gas can, I turned toward the prison, Ballard and Archer flanking me. Just three mortals about to enter a fortress of the dead.

As we passed through the rusting gate, the black walls closed in around us, making me feel more like a prisoner than a potential liberator. The buildings up ahead were drenched in menacing shadow, the heavy downpour adding to the otherworldly quality of the place.

As I blinked the rain away, I caught sporadic glimpses of ghostly figures. I'd given Skulick the *Seal of Solomon* in the hopes it would prevent Engelman from harming him, but now I missed my protective talisman. Without it, I was all too susceptible to the psychic forces around me.

I took a deep breath, shook off the vision, and kept advancing. Archer shot me a concerned look but didn't say anything. The heavy, electrically charged atmosphere discouraged all conversation. Archer and Ballard might not be able to see the dead, but they could feel them on an animal, instinctual level as we entered the main structure.

Working from memory, I made my way toward the execution chamber. I tried to not dwell on my surroundings and instead focused on the ritual ahead. I had performed exorcisms before under my partner's far more experienced and ever critical eye. This time I was flying solo. Good thing I was highly motivated to succeed. If I blew this, Archer would become the dead killer's next victim. I couldn't let that happen.

As we made our way toward the chamber where Engelman had died, I kept stealing glances at the haunting figures trapped behind the rusting cell bars. Boneless faces peered from the shadows, bloodshot eyes tracking us. Hushed, hissing whispers, guttural and inhuman, cut through the air. Our presence was stirring up these restless spirits, whipping them into a frenzy. I kept picking up one word again and again as I strode past these shadowy entities:

Innocent... Innocent... Innocent!

They repeated the word incessantly, a relentless, chilling mantra. Why was I surprised? Most prisoners believed themselves innocent in life, so why should it change in death? I envied Archer and Ballard for not being cursed with the ability to see and hear the denizens of the world beyond. My hand gripped *Hellseeker*, the bones of my knuckles sharply outlined against my skin.

"What's going on, Raven?" Archer asked. She chuckled weakly and added, "You look like you've seen a ghost."

"And they see us," I said. I tried to keep my voice steady as the anguished howls assaulted my sixth sense.

No need to scare the detectives even more. Unfortunately, the chants of the dead were getting louder around us, the entities growing more visible and substantial with each passing second.

They're drawn to me, I realized, *feeding off my psychic energy, growing stronger and more daring. Only a matter of time before they lash out at the three intruders in their midst...*

Almost as if the spirits could read my mind, the world around me changed in a flash of spiritual energy. One moment I was in the burned-down prison; the next I stood inside a burning inferno, the blackened hallways transformed into an ocean of fire, almost as if I'd accidentally taken a wrong turn into Hell itself. A blaring, insistent alarm blasted through the prison, loud enough to be heard over the roaring flames. A couple of guards surged past me, running for their lives. Poor bastards. Nobody was making it out of here alive. Everywhere I turned, inmates desperately clawed at iron bars, screaming at the top of their lungs to be let out of their cages.

The horror of the situation sickened me to the core. Smoke filled my lungs—or at least my vision convinced me it was happening—and I stumbled, leaning against Archer. Up ahead, another bellowing cry of agony rippled down the corridor. A burning inmate lurched toward me in a mad dash, face a raw mass of bubbling flesh and...

...reality snapped back to the present.

Once again, the structure was deserted, the sooth-covered walls the only reminder of the fire that had claimed so many lives.

My hands were shaking. I had to control my fear. It was feeding the dead, making them stronger. I could almost hear Skulick's voice in my head: *You swore to protect the living from the dead, mortals from monsters, so do your goddamn job!*

I pulled myself together best I could and took that next step.

And the next.

The execution chamber loomed at the end of the hallway. With every step, the hellish chorus of the damned grew louder. Even though I was here to help these spirits move to the next world, some of them clearly weren't ready to face whatever judgment awaited them in the afterlife. I wondered what Morgal had to gain from keeping these spirits bound to this forsaken prison. I answered my own question almost at once, and the idea made me sick to my stomach.

He is feasting on their suffering the way Engelman now

feeds on the souls of the living. These inmates were reliving their fiery deaths, caught in a horrific cycle from which there was no escape.

Until now.

I was about to break the cycle.

Determination growing within me, I stepped into the execution chamber.

"Wow, it's freezing in here!" Archer said.

I had braced myself for the unnatural temperature drop but still struggled not to shiver.

Ballard walked over to stand beside us. "Geez, it's like a meat locker."

"So this is it, right? We destroy this chair and poof, Engelman and his spirit army disappear," Archer said.

"That's what I'm hoping for."

It was time to get to work.

I circled the chair, mentally preparing myself for what lay ahead. Armed with the knowledge that Morgal's demonic power protected the execution device, I would break the demon's hold on this forsaken way station between life and death.

I removed a small satchel from my coat. Saying ancient prayers in a mix of Latin and Aramaic, I used the powdery substance in the satchel to lay down a protective circle around the electric chair.

Archer peered over my shoulder. "What's that?"

"You don't want to know."

The powder I was sprinkling around the chair without much enthusiasm happened to be human bone dust made from the remains of a medieval saint. It was a grisly detail best left undiscussed.

Circle complete, I removed a small dagger and drew a line of red across my hand.

I clenched my teeth as blood dribbled onto the chair. I ignored the discomfort and moved on to the next part of the ritual. Using my own blood, I drew an inverted version of Morgal's sigil on the seat of the chair.

I was almost done now. Only a final incantation remained before I would begin sprinkling gasoline over the chair and light the vile thing on fire. If I'd done my job right, the chair would be destroyed and the ghosts would cross over for good this time.

If I'd screwed up even the tiniest detail, however... well, let's just say that Blackwell Penitentiary would get three new permanent inmates.

The spirits seemed to sense what I was up to. Outside the execution chamber, the lamentations of the dead grew in volume, building into a deafening chorus. I heard wails for mercy, protestations of innocence, vicious insults, and unless I was mistaken, a pathetic cry for mommy. Most of them didn't even know that they were dead, driven by murky memories, unwilling to accept that they no longer belonged to this world.

"You guys might want to take a step back," I said, waving the detectives away from the circle.

The walls of the execution chamber shook and shivered as the psychic energy trapped here exerted a strange pressure. Archer traded a worried glance with me. The prison wasn't going to release its unholy tenants without a fight.

"Hang on," I said. "I have a feeling this might get ugly."

Ready to put an end to this nightmare, I snatched the fuel tank I'd brought along and emptied its contents on the chair. The toxic smell of gas filled my lungs as it soaked deep into the wood. Slowly, carefully, I reached for my lighter.

Unfortunately, I was so focused on the dead closing in on us from outside that I forgot to pay attention to the living.

"Raven, watch out!" Archer yelled.

Her scream was followed by the sound of a pistol being cocked.

I spun around just in time to see Ballard level his service revolver at me. The man's expression was mask-like, unreadable in the dull light of his flashlight, but his grip on the gun rock steady. Even if I hadn't seen Ballard in action back at the range, I would have known this wasn't a man who missed his target. His icy eyes glittered in the shadowy light as he took a step toward me. Crazy as it might sound, being stuck in a prison full of ghostly inmates suddenly wasn't my biggest problem.

17

D rop the gun, Archer!" Ballard barked, the barrel of his pistol fixed on her. Shock flickered over her face. I didn't blame her.

"What is this, Ballard?" Archer said. Though her gun was held steady, her lips quivered.

Ballard squeezed the trigger and a bullet chipped the wall behind Archer's head.

"I said, drop your goddamn weapon. Now! Same goes for you, Raven. Don't even think of doing anything stupid. Next time I won't miss."

The sound of our pistols hitting the floor echoed in the ice-cold death chamber, eerily amplified. Ballard scooped up Archer's pistol. *Hellseeker* remained at my feet, glowing faintly. Just a matter of time before Ballard would help himself to my blessed weapon too.

"What the hell is wrong with you?" Archer yelled, her voice thick with emotion.

The question hung in the air for a beat before Ballard's lips twisted into a grin. "*Hell*. We use that word so casually nowadays. Without respect or fear of any consequences."

The man talking to us shared little in common with the nervous guy knocking back shots at my loft hours earlier. There was a brazen confidence in the way he carried himself, an air of animal cunning. This wasn't a man afraid of the dark but someone who embraced it. All this time Ballard had been wearing a carefully crafted mask, playing us for fools.

"What do you think you're doing here, Ballard?" I said. "You do realize there are ghosts in this prison that only I can see and hear. And they don't seem to like *you* too much-"

I broke off, distracted by a renewed barrage of ghostly whispers.

Innocent... Innocent... Innocent...

Tuning into the ghostly mantra, the veil lifted from my eyes. I suddenly understood. The dead were trying to communicate the same message Engelman had shared with me when our souls momentarily touched earlier.

"I was set up. I never killed anyone. I didn't do it! I'm innocent..."

As Engelman's words went once again through my mind, all the pieces clicked into place. Engelman had been telling the truth from the beginning. The professor of Comparative Religion and Occult studies had been set up for murders he never committed. Set up by one of the detectives who'd brought him to justice.

"It was you," I said, my voice humming with shocked surprise. "You set up Engelman for your murders. You're *Lucifer's Disciple*."

Ballard's chilling grin, an expression of fanatical pride, told me I was right. For the last three years, he'd allowed another man to take credit for his grisly handiwork. Like some demented artist working anonymously behind the scenes, he was elated to finally receive some recognition for his evil deeds.

"No, that's impossible," Archer gasped. "It can't be."

"I'm afraid Raven knows what he's talking about. Engelman died in this room because of *me*."

"That's impossible. I've worked with you for years..."

"And you never suspected a thing. Some kind of detective you are. But then again, I wasn't always like this."

He took a step toward Archer, and my jaw tightened.

Ballard wouldn't be confessing his crimes if he expected us to ever leave Blackwell alive.

"After the Crimson Circle caused their breach to the other side and the supernatural shit storm started to hit our city, I finally wised up. All this time, I'd been fighting for the wrong side. Mankind was doomed, headed straight toward the apocalypse. For years, I'd been trying to do the right thing, but for every bad guy I put behind bars, two new ones took his place. I could never win for one simple reason: the dark is stronger than the light. After two decades, it was time to be on the winning side."

"So you went around slaughtering innocent people and carving sick occult shit onto their bodies? You fucking freak!" Archer's voice was shaking with rage now. I didn't blame her. This was betrayal on a level I'd never experienced. It would be like finding out Skulick had secretly been working for Morgal this whole time.

"I was welcoming the darkness into my life, hoping the masters of Hell would take notice of me and accept me into their fold."

I watched Ballard carefully as he spoke. Like Desmond Horne, he was clearly a nutjob who thought he could achieve transcendence through works of evil— a man dreaming of being a monster, a mortal foolishly hoping Hell would grant him a place among their infernal ranks.

Even though his words held a strange, dark logic, I wasn't buying it. It seemed more like Ballard was desperately trying to rationalize what he'd become. He might try to convince himself that the years of battling crime had burned him out. I saw it differently. Evil hadn't worn him out; it had seduced him. It had probably started with something small. A bribe accepted in exchange for looking the other way, removing drugs from evidence for an additional payday—who knew what exactly had set him on this twisted, murderous path? With time, he had allowed the darkness into his heart, allowed it to infect him and ultimately claim his soul.

I'd seen it all before. Every twisted sorcerer I'd put down over the years had started the same way. Just one little spell, a minor deal with the forces of darkness to make life a little sweeter. Inevitably, infernal power corrupted. Ballard was just one more sucker who'd fallen for Hell's phony promises.

The breach between our world and the world of monsters hadn't been the beginning of his twisted journey—it had signaled the end. He was too far gone to save.

My cold glare fixed on him as I spoke. "If you were so determined to join the forces of Hell, why pin it on

Engelman? Why let an innocent man pay for your sick crimes?"

Ballard met my gaze with a glassy-eyed stare, head tilted slightly to one side, almost as if he was wondering whether he owed me an explanation at all. Even monsters want to be understood on some level, and he couldn't resist telling me all about his scheme.

"I went to every one of Engelman's lectures, read all his books but his insights into the paranormal turned out to be lies. No matter how many souls I offered to my dark masters, I remained invisible to them, an insect unworthy of their attention. The demons never revealed themselves, refusing to answer my calls."

He sounded for all the world like a frustrated high school kid who couldn't get the prom queen to notice him. It would have been pathetic if he wasn't about to kill us. Ballard's gun never wavered as he circled me and Archer, his body infused with a nervous energy. He wasn't merely telling us his story; he was reliving every single moment.

"When my efforts failed to elicit a response from Hell, I started to question myself. Maybe I was wrong, maybe I was even crazy. All great men will face periods of crushing self-doubt. With my rituals failing and the cops closing in, I needed to buy myself more time."

"So you got yourself assigned to the investigation,"

Archer said. "You targeted Engelman's students, planted evidence linking him to the murders. You set up an innocent man for your crimes, you sick freak."

"It's your own fault, Archer. If you hadn't been so determined to catch your man, Engelman might still be alive."

Archer's eyes narrowed, mouth pressed into a thin line.

"Sounds like someone got scared. Was the thought of ending up in the electric chair keeping you up at night?"

What was Archer doing? Was she baiting Ballard? Didn't she realize she was facing a psycho with a gun pointing at her.

But Jane was beyond reason. The anger at being betrayed by her old partner had taken hold of her.

"I know why your twisted rituals failed. Hell hates a fucking coward!"

Without warning, Ballard viciously brought the butt of his pistol down on Archer. She let out a muffled cry and crumpled. Ballard kicked her for good measure.

Something in me snapped. Seeing red, I threw caution to the wind and lunged at Ballard. I didn't give a shit about the pistol in his hand, didn't give a shit about my own safety. Only Archer mattered. And this beast was hurting her...

I was almost upon him when the barrel of his firearm swiveled toward Archer, kissing her forehead.

Despite my boiling rage, I froze, less than three feet between us now. One wrong move on my part and he would drill a bullet into Archer's head.

"Back the fuck off! Now!"

Reluctantly I complied, my gaze never leaving Archer. She was on the ground, bloodied but her eyes had not lost her fighting spirit.

"Get in the chair!" Ballard ordered.

Once again, the pistol fixed on Archer left me no choice. I had to play along for now.

"If you try anything again, I'll shoot this bitch in the fucking face. Now get in the chair, Raven."

Eyes never leaving Ballard, I did as I was told. A chill tore up my spine as my back leaned into the gasoline-soaked wooden chair, the scar on my chest coming to life. The chair was stained with old evil, marked by pain. How many monsters had exited this world in this contraption, fifty thousand volts surging through flesh and bone?

Ballard eased closer, gun trained on me. A groggy Archer watched helplessly as her former partner began to tighten the chair's straps around my hands. Gasoline stained my coat, and I fought valiantly to stave off my growing panic.

Stop it and think! There has to be a way out! There always is!

Ballard secured a thick strap around my midsection. My chest heaved and strained against the leather band, and it cost me a considerable amount of willpower to normalize my breathing. The fumes from the fuel weren't helping matters, stinging my eyes and throat.

"What are you doing?" I asked, fighting back the cough building in my throat. I wanted to keep Ballard talking while I figured a way out of this mess. Once I was out of the picture, Ballard's attention would be directed at his old partner. And I had a feeling that with Archer, he would take his sweet time.

Ballard finished securing a second strap around my waist and said, "I can admit it. The demons I worshipped felt me unworthy of their attention. And for good reason. I wasn't ready. But this time around, things will be different. This time my call will be answered. The last few hours have shown me I was on the right path all along. Engelman's published work might have been lies, but clearly he was holding back the good stuff. I merely lacked the right knowledge. The right sacrifice."

When he said *sacrifice*, Ballard was talking about yours truly. I was at the top of Hell's most wanted list, and Ballard planned to deliver me on a platter to the Prince of Darkness.

Fool! Ballard erroneously believed he could buy his way into Hell. The bastard was due for a rude awakening. The Prince of Darkness wasn't known for his sense of gratitude or a willingness to reward his unholy servants. Far from it.

"Ballard, you *are* crazy," I said. "Demons are liars and double-crossers. You're a fool if you think you can bargain with them and walk away the winner."

Ballard glowered at me. "We'll see about that."

He took a step closer. "And one more thing before I forget. Once I'm done here, I'm going to head back to your warehouse, put your crippled partner out of his misery and help myself to the secrets of your library."

For a moment, it felt like Ballard had flicked a switch and brought the electric chair to life, his words sizzling through me. Skulick was well-protected against supernatural threats, thanks to the *Seal of Solomon*, but his mystical defenses wouldn't deflect a bullet. I had to stop this monster.

Good call, buddy, but you need a plan.

Fast.

Unarmed and tied to an electric chair soaked in gasoline, I was fresh out of options. I'd escaped worse situations, or so I was trying to tell myself, but this time I wasn't just trying to save my own skin. I had to get Archer out of here.

I searched her bloodied face. I hated seeing her like this. What could she do without her pistol? Even if she made a suicide run at Ballard, bullets would strike her down before she could reach him. And I'd still be tied to this goddamn chair.

But maybe there was another way.

Maybe I could seek help from the lost souls trapped within these accursed walls.

Engelman had made a pact with Morgal so he could return from the grave and prove his innocence. Naturally, the demon had tricked him, trapping his soul with the monsters in this prison so that their evil and rage would infect him. But many innocent people had been caught in the web of the ritual, and those imprisoned souls had to be desperate to escape their earthbound purgatory.

Focusing my sixth sense was more difficult than usual, what with the fear of imminent death, but I managed to send out some psychic feelers. I pictured Ballard's face in my mind until I could see every detail of the detective's rugged features.

This is the man who is responsible for your suffering, I thought, *the man who is trying to keep you imprisoned.*

At first there was no indication that I was reaching my intended audience but soon the chants of the damned began to change. Their whispers now echoed in my head.

Guilty! Guilty! Guilty!

My message was getting through, filling the minds of the doomed spirits housed within this prison. And with each passing second, their mantra grew in intensity and volume.

Ballard was busy securing my legs to the chair, completely unaware of the chaos building around us. As he tightened the last belt securing me to the death chair, he leaned forward and patted me on the shoulder.

"Sorry, but I can't risk you running around this place once I set you on fire. It might disturb the locals."

How nice, a considerate psychopath.

He flashed me a grin. The bastard thought he was funny, too, but there was only room enough in the cursed city for one charmingly sarcastic bastard. My sudden preternatural calm combined with the confident sparkle in my eyes visibly unnerved him. I was too cool for a man who was about to barbecued alive.

I decided to press my momentary advantage and knock him farther off balance. "You know why Hell never showed itself to you, Ballard? The Prince of Darkness can spot a rank amateur a mile away."

Rage crept into Ballard's gaze, but he caught himself

before rising to my taunt. Instead he pocketed one of the pistols and extricated a lighter from his jacket.

"Let's see if I can wipe that cocky grin off your face."

And with those words, Ballard flicked the lighter, spark turning to flame, and my world transformed into a searing inferno.

18

Ravenous flames engulfed the chair, threatening to turn me into a human torch. The fact that my clothes were still soaked from the rain would buy me only a couple of seconds.

Then, a violent blast of air roared through the death chamber, extinguishing the burgeoning blaze. Choking back toxic smoke, my eyes tearing, I vaguely made out my saviors. A ring of entities had appeared at the far edge of the execution chamber. Guards, prison employees, even a few inmates. Hate-filled eyes bored into Ballard.

A beat later, the leather straps securing me to the blackened chair snapped and tore, and I was free. I had no doubt that my spectral rescuers were responsible for this Houdini act. Ballard stared at me with wild eyes, his mouth hanging open in shock.

I, on the other hand, was ready to make my move.

My clothes still smoking – thanks for ruining a perfectly good coat, asshole – I bolted out of the chair and launched myself at Ballard.

I slammed into the sick bastard and we both went down in a mass of flailing limbs. We rolled across the floor, locked in a fierce wrestling match. It would've been nice for the ghosts to come to my aid, but it seemed these entities had already exerted whatever energy they could muster. It was up to me now to finish this business.

A sharp pain tore through my skull as Ballard's elbow found my chin. Two more punches rained down, and I exhaled sharply, spitting blood. While I was still recovering from the flurry of blows, Ballard head-butted me full force. My nose seemed to explode. As I groggily tried to regain my senses, Ballard jumped to his feet and scooped up the pistols he'd dropped during my attack.

A gunshot tore through the execution chamber.

I flinched, but I wasn't the one who'd been hit. During my brawl with psycho-boy, Archer had helped herself to *Hellseeker* and managed to squeeze off a shot. The blessed weapon was capable of inflicting damage on the dead as well as the living.

Ballard returned fire while staggering out of the death chamber and Archer went down. A moment later, Ballard had vanished through the exit, leaving me and Archer behind.

For an eternal moment, I remained frozen in place, gun smoke wafting around me. The coppery flavor of my own blood numbed my mouth. I'd faced indescribable horrors over the years, battled monsters and demons, but I'd never felt such dread as when I saw the woman I love hit the floor.

Okay, I admit it. I love her. I'm crazy about Detective Jane Archer.

And now she was lying in a pool of her own blood. I crawled toward her, desperately hoping that the the damage wasn't as bad as it looked. As I approached, she glanced up at me with big eyes. Her shirt was stained scarlet, but her grip was strong as she snatched my hand. Even with a bullet or two in her, Archer still had the spunk of a born fighter.

I inspected the wound. The bleeding appeared to be coming from her arm. Thank God, Ballard appeared to have missed any vital organs.

"Are you alright, babe?"

"Who you calling babe? Ouch, this shit hurts..."

I grinned like an idiot at the sound of her voice. Even down for the count, she was still a fighter.

"Get that fucker. I'll be alright!"

I squeezed her hand, hating myself for leaving her behind in the execution chamber but knowing someone had to put an end to Ballard. Snatching *Hellseeker* from where Archer had dropped the weapon during her shootout with Ballard, I jumped back to my feet and tore out of the execution chamber.

A dark hallway lined with empty holding cells awaited me.

I advanced slowly, knowing the enemy might wait around any corner. Somewhere in the pools of corpse-gray moonlight was Ballard. I swore he wouldn't get far.

I cast out with my sixth sense, hoping that the ghosts might be able to guide me, but I picked up nothing. Morgal's scar had made me receptive to the other side, but I wasn't a full-blown psychic like Joe Cormac.

Hellseeker ready, I continued down the dimly lit corridor, following the trail of blood Ballard had left behind. Archer had hit the man, that much was certain. I generally used lethal force against monsters, not mortal men. But today I would make an exception.

I reached the end of the cellblock and trailed the line of scarlet down a steel staircase. Rage simmered inside me as my shoes clanged down the steps.

I spotted Ballard moments later. He stood in the center of the main hall, surrounded by three floors of prison cells on all sides. His gun was down and his body hunched over, and he appeared smaller than he had only a few minutes ago. Was it merely blood loss, or was something else affecting the detective?

Lucifer's So-Called Disciple barely paid me any attention, his gaze riveted to the rows of prison cells which encircled us both. I followed his gaze and stifled a gasp.

Frank Engelman had arrived at Blackwell!

The former professor of the occult stood on the second floor of the penitentiary, and his band of psychopaths had formed an impenetrable spectral wall around us.

By saving my life, the lost souls in the prison had interrupted the exorcism ritual. The chair would need to fully burn down to send Engelman and the other spirits packing. Blinded by my anger, I'd forgotten why we had come to Blackwell in the first place—stopping the soul-eating entity looming menacingly above us. By allowing this fight to become personal, I had sacrificed our best way of defeating Engelman.

Another thought occurred to me. How was Ballard able to see the ghosts?

They want him to see them. Want him to feel their pain and rage. Want him to be as afraid as they were on that night when the fire took them.

The band of ghosts began to circle Ballard, inexorably zeroing in on their prey. Ballard backed away, his eyes alive with terror. Archer had seen right through this monster—Ballard was a coward.

"Raven, you have to help me. How do we stop them?"

We don't.

Even if I could've, I wouldn't have helped the sick bastard.

Engelman and his spirit army drew closer and closer until they were upon Ballard.

"Get away from me! I killed you, Engelman! You're dead!"

And so are you, buddy.

I watched in grim silence as they viciously tore into Lucifer's Disciple. More like Lucifer's Embarrassment. I felt numb, beyond emotion. The less I talk about what happened next the better. Let's just say that very little of Ballard was left by the time they were done with him. Gore caked the floor, and I was glad I'd skipped dinner.

And lunch.

Their need for vengeance satiated, the dead prisoners now turned their attention toward me. To my horror, I spotted one new addition to their ranks. Ballard. Of course. Anyone who perished within these walls would be trapped in the same manner as all the other inmates. Even though the first phase of my exorcism spell had removed the glyphs from the chair, the dark magic remained embedded in the structure itself. Until someone fully incinerated the electric chair, this evil would persist.

Ballard flanked Engelman as the spectral entities homed in on me. I didn't need to steal another glance at Ballard's unrecognizable remains to know what these monsters had in store for me.

19

The smell of fire and ash woke Joe Cormac from his latest blackout. For a confusing moment, he thought he was in Iraq, but this moldy, damp air shared little in common with the bone-dry heat of the desert country that had tried to kill him. As he soaked in the rows of holding cells, he knew he was back where it had all started. Blackwell Penitentiary. Why would Engelman return to this forsaken place?

To stop Raven!

The fractured memories of the spirit's plan swirled through his brain like psychic shrapnel. Engelman was here to prevent Raven from doing something...but what? When Engelman possessed him, their psychic link went both ways. The fiend could look into his soul but sometimes he caught glimpses too. He racked his brain but failed to recall any details. The splitting headache wasn't helping matters. Each time Engelman took possession of him, the pain grew worse.

He is draining you, sucking you dry like all his other victims.

Joe massaged his throbbing skull. He doubted he'd live through Engelman's next mental assault. One way or another, this ordeal ended tonight. Bones creaked and sore muscles protested as he staggered to his feet. While he struggled to maintain his balance, another question cycled through his mind. Had it been hours or days since the incident at Raven's loft? There was no way to tell. Time had lost all meaning to him at this point, his life before Blackwell like a distant dream.

Gingerly, he started to explore the prison. Shadows pooled around him, the darkness seemingly alive. Joe felt no fear. He was beyond emotion at this point. Engelman had turned his soul inside out, transformed him into a shell of the man he once was. His body aching all over, he stumbled through the rotting structure that, once upon a time, had housed so many monsters.

He didn't get far.

A few feet down the next corridor, Joe froze in place, almost forgetting to exhale. Up ahead, at the center of the main prison floor, the spirits of the dead had surrounded Raven.

There was nothing he could do to save the monster hunter now. He couldn't save anyone, not even himself.

The execution chamber!

Unbidden, the thought ripped through his mind. Joe had first encountered Engelman in the death chamber. Perhaps it also held the key to defeating the undead fiend.

As Joe retraced his steps from memory, stumbling toward a nearby staircase, the phalanx of ghosts paid him no mind, their attention riveted on Raven.

Once Joe reached the prison's third level, he didn't bother to look down at the main floor. The monster hunter could handle himself. Or not. Joe was past caring.

When he finally arrived in the execution room, his gaze landed on the bleeding woman sprawled on the floor. She stared back at him in surprise but said nothing, her jaw clenched with evident pain.

Although Joe had never met the woman before, he recognized her immediately. Her name was Jane Archer. One of Engelman's targets. And she was barely conscious and fading fast.

"Don't be afraid," he said, trying to sound reassuring. Joe had been a hero once, hadn't he? He vaguely remembered a time in his life when he'd fought a war to keep his country safe. "I'm here to help."

Noble words, but would he be able to back them up with action? He scanned the chamber. Something had changed. The electric chair was smoking, the wood singed...

He finally understood why Raven had returned to the prison. He'd come back here to destroy the chair. But something or someone had interrupted the process.

His chest tight with determination, Joe advanced toward the electric chair. He would finish what Raven had begun.

The time had come to send Engelman to Hell.

"The lighter," the woman croaked.

She was pointing weakly at the metal lighter near the chair. Judging by the trail of blood behind her, she's been dragging her wounded body toward it.

Joe nodded.

He scooped up the Zippo.

And then, for the second time that day, the electric chair burned.

20

A n army of the dead encircled me.

For a moment, the spectral horde stood in tableau, almost as if they were tuned into some extrasensory frequency.

They're waiting for Engelman to give them permission to attack, I thought.

The pack expecting the alpha to issue the kill order.

They didn't have to wait for too long.

Lips widening in howls of murderous rage, the ghosts closed in on me in jerky bursts of motion. There was nowhere to run, nowhere to hide. I'd foolishly hoped Ballard's death might satiate Engelman's murderous impulses. Unfortunately, the desire to clear his name had set the former professor on a monstrous path from which there was no turning back.

Piece of advice: Allying yourself with a demon like Morgal never ended well.

The evil of Blackwell Penitentiary had infected the innocent man, his soul darkened and corrupted by the rot of this place. Hoping to expose a monster, he'd become one himself. Unless I stopped Engelman here and now, the killings would continue.

Still, I tried to reach him and his ghostly followers. "You don't have to remain trapped here anymore," I cried out. "You can finally be a peace. All of you! Let me help you."

For a beat, Engelman paused. Hope flared in my soul, but it was short-lived.

Engelman's black eyes blazed with a supernatural fire, bereft of all humanity. And then the spirit spoke, the words coming haltingly.

"SOON IT WILL ALL BE OVER! No more death. No more life. No more pain."

"That's nice," I muttered. Amazingly enough, Engelman's sales pitch wasn't winning me over. There was only one option left to me. Could I shoot my way through this spectral horde and make it back to the execution chamber in time to complete the ritual? I thought of Archer bleeding out in the death chamber and knew I had to try.

Gnashing my teeth, I brought up *Hellseeker*. It was

time for the magical pistol to live up to its name. A barrage of blessed lead descended on the first wave of entities. Each bullet found its target, shattering spectral forms into tendrils of white hot energy and ectoplasm.

It was a temporary reprieve at best. Experience had taught me that *Hellseeker* couldn't solve this problem, but hopefully it would allow me to carve a path through the wailing wall of wraiths.

I moved and fired at the same time, a man possessed by love and fear and all those other squishy emotions that make us human, adrenaline roaring through my veins. The shrieks of the damned pounded against my eardrums, and I had to avert my eyes from their horrifically distorted faces.

Next to me, the steel door of a prison cell was brutally torn off by a ghostly force. I ducked as the door-turned-deadly-projectile hurled toward me. It sailed over my head and smashed into a nearby wall, plaster showering down on me.

No time to dwell on the attempted decapitation as more ghosts lunged at me. I drilled bullets into the first three, their forms writhing and disintegrating.

I kept battling my way to the staircase that would lead me back to the third floor, back to the execution chamber.

I almost made it.

Almost.

Engelman materialized right in front of me just as I reached the bottom step. Before I could react, the ghost's arm shot out at me, eerily elongating in mid-attack. A spectral fist dipped into my chest, and I felt cold fingers close around my beating heart.

No!

My pistol came up, the green glowing barrel of *Hellseeker* finding Engelman's shimmering forehead. I squeezed and...

Nothing happened.

Out of ammo.

I'm sorry, Archer, I failed you.

I blinked away the morose thoughts and glared back at Engelman, unwilling to give him the satisfaction of seeing me mentally defeated.

And that's when Engelman was jerked back by a phantom force, his hand yanking out of my chest in a cold rush of energy. The spirit recoiled, his whole body trembling and shaking, lashed by some invisible force. Almost as if thousands of volts of electricity were passing through him...

With a roar of agony, Engelman's body began to evaporate. His features were the last to disappear. During that final moment, his gaze cleared, his madness lifted, restored to the man he'd been while alive. Reading his lips, I made out his final words: *Thank You.*

I wasn't the one who deserved his gratitude. Someone else had put Engelman out of his misery.

The other ghosts began to ignite around me. Spectral flames enveloped the entities, hungrily devouring long-dead flesh.

Understanding dawned. The inmates were reliving their final moments, but this time they would stay dead. It seemed like the ghosts were exiting this plane in the order they had perished, first Engelman, then the inmates and guards who'd died in the fire.

Ballard watched in shocked surprise as the specters continued to go up in flames around him. He would be the last one to exit this world if my theory held true. I drew some satisfaction that even in death, Ballard would be denied that which the twisted freak desired most—a chance at a private audience with his demonic masters. The forces of darkness have little tolerance or patience for failure.

The number of burning spirits was shrinking rapidly. One by one, the specters went supernova and fused into a powerful stream of supernatural energy. Blinding white light washed over me.

I averted my eyes. I knew better than to stare too

long into the light. Where those spirits were going, I had
no desire to follow.

Suddenly my blood turned cold. I'd spotted the
arrival of a new figure on the third floor.

I held up a hand, waving to get her attention. "Hey,
Archer, you're late to the party," I called out.

She didn't answer.

She didn't even look at me.

My heart hitched in my throat as I realized what was
wrong. Her eyes were glassy, unfocused, and she looked
pale and washed-out. No, not just pale--translucent. I
could actually see the brick wall through her wavering
form.

That wasn't Archer.

It was her ghost.

21

With agonizing slowness, Archer's gaze turned to me. For an eternal moment, our eyes met across the prison's sea of burning bodies. Plenty of things had kept us apart—not least my own boneheaded stupidity—but now the vast gulf between life and death separated us.

For most of my adult life, I'd kept people at arm's length. I'd told myself that if I cared for someone, I would be putting them in danger. And so I'd slammed the door on every chance of happiness. With Archer, I'd found someone who knew who I was and what I did and wasn't afraid to stand by my side. But instead of holding on tight and promising to never let go, I'd turned my back on her.

For a man who fought demons, I was certainly a coward.

Maybe in some recess of my mind, some shadowy corner of my heart, I had believed we would find a way to make it work in some distant future when evil was defeated and the last demon had been banished. But there would never be an end to this war—and I knew it. Mortals had battled monsters long before I was ever born, and they would continue to do so once I'd long passed from the world. This had never been about the risk Archer might face if we became a couple; it was always about *me*. My fear of losing someone I loved the way I lost my parents.

And now my worst nightmare had become a reality. Archer was dead. I'd left her to bleed to death, alone, on a filthy prison floor.

Ballard's ghost started screaming as he relived his death. In moments, his spirit would cross over, and then it would be Archer's turn. She'd be gone forever. I couldn't let that happen.

As her form started to judder, my body exploded into motion. I tore up the staircase, taking two steps at a time. My heart and soul were a mass of exposed nerve endings as I barreled down the corridor into the execution chamber.

The stench of burned wood and leather greeted me.

The electric chair had been reduced to a pile of ash and blackened fastenings. Joe Cormac, still alive but looking as though he'd aged several decades in the last week, was crouched beside Archer's body. His eyes met mine, and he shook his head, just once.

Fighting back tears of rage and pain, I dropped to my knees at her side. Joe Cormac tried to reach out to me but I roughly shoved his hand aside.

"I'm sorry. I tried to help her...." His voice helplessly trailed off.

I gingerly felt for a pulse. Nothing. It didn't make sense. The wound in her shoulder must have hurt, but it shouldn't have killed her. I leaned in closer and that's when I discovered a second bullet wound, previously hidden under Archer's leather jacket. Black blood seeped from it. The bullet must've hit her liver, a death sentence even if, by some miracle, I should manage to revive her.

Ignoring logic, I began to perform CPR. As I blew precious oxygen into Archer's mouth and pounded her chest, hoping to jolt her heart back into motion, her forlorn spirit appeared before me, eyes filled with fear and shock. To see the brave detective like that broke whatever was left of my heart. *Don't worry, babe, I won't let you go this time. I swear.*

With each breath I shared with Archer, her spirit

drew closer. Was the CPR working? Encouraged, I increased my efforts.

With an eerie psychic wail that made both me and Joe Cormac clap our hands over our ears, Archer's spirit was dragged back into her broken body.

Archer's eyelids flickered, her fists clenched, and a violent, choking cough escaped from her throat as she drew her first breath since her heart had given out. She was back among the living, spirit and body reunited. Fearful eyes looked up at me as she coughed again, her lips bloody. I had managed to bring her back...but for how long? Had I merely sentenced Archer to more suffering until her organs finally gave out again? Could even the best hospital in the world save her at this point?

Modern medicine might not be able to heal her wounds—but *I* could. What was the point in safeguarding a treasure trove of magical objects if I couldn't use them for a noble cause? And what could be more noble than saving the woman I loved from an untimely death?

My mind working a mile a minute, I jumped to my feet and scooped up the detective. God, she felt so cold. I lurched out of the death chamber with her in my arms. It must've looked like the cover of some demented romance novel-a beautiful woman fainting in my arms as I carried her out of Hell. Joe Cormac, old before his time and hobbling silently behind us, sort of ruined the picture. As did the fact we were all covered in blood and soot.

In hindsight, I admit that I wasn't thinking completely rationally at the time. My soul felt like a hemorrhaging wound, and I was willing to throw caution to the wind and break every rule if it meant Archer would be spared from the Grim Reaper.

Somehow, I managed to find my way out of the prison. Lightning flashed and thunder rattled as I stepped into the rain-swept night.

I opened the passenger door to the Equus Bass and lowered Archer into the seat as gently as I could, heedless of the gore now staining the upholstery. The car could be replaced. Archer was one of a kind.

I slammed the door shut and staggered toward the driver's side, nearly slipping on the soaked ground. As I yanked open the door, my gaze landed on the prison one last time. Cormac fronted the rusting main entrance, wet clothes sticking to him like a second skin. He was staring, not at me but at the roof of the building, one bony hand pointing upward. A winged, shadowy shape stood revealed in a flash of lightning.

Morgal.

The demon lurked on the high penitentiary walls like some demented gargoyle, bat-like wings extended, a terrifying image in the sickly light. His booming laughter, hollow and eerie, resounded through the night, managing to even drown out the sounds of the storm. The demon was mocking me, reminding me that while I might have beaten him, victory had come at an excruciatingly high price.

By the time the next flash of lightning lit up the night, the demon was long gone, briefly making me wonder if perhaps I'd imagined the whole thing. The dark expression in Cormac's eyes convinced me otherwise.

I dragged my gaze away from the prison of horror and got in the car. One hand reached out for Archer and gently touched her arm, almost as though I needed to reassure myself she was still here, as I started the engine. I prayed Archer would be able to hold on long enough for me to reach the loft. Although I'm ashamed to admit it, I didn't worry about Cormac too much. The car that had been parked next to mine would get him safely back to the city.

Tires skidded on wet pavement, visibility reduced to shit. Outside, heavy wind gusted the whipping rain. The monotonous thump of wipers the only sound in the car, the world behind the windshield nothing more than a shadowy dream.

I lost track of time as I drove, my body on autopilot as my mind churned. When I finally reached my loft, I pulled Archer from the car as carefully as I could. I barely remember making my way into the elevator and keying in my entry code. There was no sign of Skulick. He was probably still being questioned downtown, and I felt secretly glad. If Skulick wasn't here, he couldn't tell me not go through with my plan.

I was headed for the vault. The ward-protected chamber contained the most dangerous mystical items Skulick and I had secured over the years.

I gently lowered Archer to the floor and punched another secret code into the keypad. The door rumbled open. A beat later, I entered the windowless, silver-reinforced vault. Occult items lined the walls, a museum of the bizarre. As always the collection of cursed items called out to me, but I blocked the steady stream of eerie whispers.

Luckily, I was beyond temptation at this point. I knew exactly what I was looking for.

I homed in on a chalice made from gold and adorned with a series of strange engravings. A similarly adorned seal covered the top of the cup, offering no hint as to its contents, but something sloshed inside when I picked it up. As my fingers closed around the grail, I could hear Skulick's gruff voice inside my head, telling me to reconsider what I was about to do. I refused to listen. It wouldn't exactly be the first time I'd ignored the old man's advice. All that mattered was saving Archer.

Grail in hand, I stepped out of the vault and knelt beside Archer. I patted her face and called out her name. Archer wouldn't wake up. Cursing myself, I pressed my thumb against the bullet wound on her shoulder.

Archer screamed. I cradled her against my chest, murmuring soothing nonsense until she calmed down. She weakly blinked at me, her eyes wide and confused.

"Raven? Where—"

A thin line of blood trickled from her mouth.

"Hush now, just drink."

I tilted the cup toward her lips and poured the dark liquid down her throat. For a torturous moment, nothing happened. And then I felt the change.

Color returned to Archer's drained features, her grip around my arm growing stronger. Her eyes fluttered open and locked on me. I looked down at her torn shirt and almost grinned. The bullet hole was closing up, healing itself before my eyes.

I clung to her as the magic of the grail repaired her wounds.

Don't ask me how long it took. All I know is that I felt like a man waking from a dream when Archer shoved me away and sprang to her feet. The notion that her life had ever been in danger would have felt like a surreal nightmare if it hadn't been for all the blood on her shirt. I stood up and reached out for her, laughing in stupid, exhausted relief. I'd done it. She was back.

Archer took a step toward me.

I did the same.

And then we kissed, our lips finding each other. Her mouth was soft, but it tasted like blood.

I didn't care. Archer was alive and in my arms.

Then a bolt of pain shot through the mark on my chest. I gasped and took a step back. Archer blinked at me, uncomprehending. "What is it, Mike?"

The question still hung in the air as a sharp spasm wracked her. She cried out with agony and her legs buckled.

As tremors passed through Archer's body, I watched in frozen, helpless horror.

When she finally looked up at me again, I knew that I would be damned for what I'd done to her tonight.

I should have let her go.

Oh God, I should have let her die.

The woman staring back at me looked like Jane Archer, but her skin was deathly pale and twin fangs dimpled her bottom lip. Lightning fast, her hand gripped my wrist with superhuman strength. A second later, she was on top of me, fangs about to bury themselves into my throat. I barely resisted. I deserved whatever damnation was waiting for me.

But something stopped her. Clarity washed over those animalistic eyes, and she backed away.

I instinctively reached for her.

"STAY AWAY FROM ME!"

With a feral roar, she ran, her gaze wild, her movements jerky and explosive. Before I could react, she darted toward the nearest skylight and hurled herself through the window. Glass shattered, and so did my world. I ran to the broken window and peered into the rainy night. There was no sign of Archer. The darkness had swallowed her whole.

A sound behind me made me whirl.

Skulick's wheelchair was buzzing toward me. His sharp eyes moved from my face to the empty grail near my feet and the destroyed window, putting the pieces together.

"What have you done?" Skulick said, his voice shaking with accusation.

As I struggled to respond, I knew nothing would

ever be the same again. I'd broken my partner's trust in the worst possible way by using the blood of a vampire to save Archer. I'd unleashed a new monster on the cursed city. And she just happened to be the woman I loved.

NOT THE END

Mike Raven and John Skulick will return in BLOOD RAIN.

If you enjoyed this novel, please consider writing an Amazon review - they really help.

I'm an indie writer and anything you can do to get the word out to other readers is deeply appreciated. Thank you for your support and your time! You can follow this direct link below:

http://www.amazon.com/review/create-review/ref+ cm_cr_dp_wrt_btm?ie=UTF8&asin=B0IN9GY3MI

Want to get an email when the next SHADOW DETECTIVE title is released and receive a free novella? Subscribe to my newsletter!

Click here to get started: **http://eepurl.com/Ki8QH**

The Shadow Detective story continues in Blood Rain
Out Now. Grab Your Copy here!

AMAZON US

AMAZON UK

ABOUT THE AUTHOR

William Massa is a produced screenwriter and best-selling Amazon author. His film credits include *Return to House on Haunted Hill* and he has sold pitches and scripts to Warner, USA TV, Silver Pictures, Dark Castle, Maverick and Sony.

William has lived in New York, Florida, Europe and now resides in Venice Beach surrounded by skaters and surfers. He writes science fiction and dark fantasy/urban fantasy horror with an action-adventure flavor.

Writing can be a solitary pursuit but rewriting can be a group effort. I strive to make each book better than the last and feedback is incredibly helpful. If you have notes, thoughts or comments about this book or want to contact me, feel free to contact me at:

williammassabooks@gmail.com

ALSO BY WILLIAM MASSA

THE SHADOW DETECTIVE SERIES

Cursed City

Soul Catcher

Blood Rain

Demon Dawn

Skull Master

Ghoul Night

THE OCCULT ASSASSIN SERIES

Damnation Code

Apocalypse Soldier

Spirit Breaker

Soul Jacker

THE GARGOYLE KNIGHT SERIES

Gargoyle Knight

Gargoyle Quest

THE SILICON WORLD SERIES

Silicon Dawn

Silicon Man

STAND ALONES

Fear the Light

Match: A Supernatural Thriller

Crossing the Darkness

Printed in Great Britain
by Amazon

65254177R00121